The last, hazy days of August are meant for basking in the sun and reading good books. Whether you're relaxing in your backyard, on your porch or maybe chilling on vacation, make sure to have a selection of Harlequin Presents titles by your side. We've got eight great novels to choose from....

Bestselling author Lynne Graham presents her latest tale of a mistress who's forced to marry an Italian billionaire in *Mistress Bought and Paid For*. And Miranda Lee is as steamy as ever with her long-awaited romp, *Love-Slave to the Sheikh*, for our hot UNCUT miniseries.

You never know what goes on behind closed doors, and we have three very different stories about marriages to prove it: Anne Mather's sexy and emotional *Jack Riordan's Baby* will have your heart in your mouth while also tugging at its strings, while *Bought by Her Husband*, Sharon Kendrick's newest release, and Kate Walker's *The Antonakos Marriage* are two slices of Greek tycoon heaven with spicy twists!

If it's something more traditional you're after, we've plenty of choice: *By Royal Demand*, the first installment in Robyn Donald's new regal saga, THE ROYAL HOUSE OF ILLYRIA, won't disappoint. Or you might like to try *The Italian Millionaire's Virgin Wife* by Diana Hamilton and *His Very Personal Assistant* by Carole Mortimer—two shy, sensible, prim-and-proper women find themselves living lives they've never dreamed of when they attract two rich, arrogant and darkly handsome men!

Enjoy!

*Legally wed,
but he's never said,
"I love you."
They're...*

*The series where marriages are made
in haste...and love comes later....*

*Look out for more WEDLOCKED!
wedding stories available only from
Harlequin Presents®.*

Anne Mather

JACK RIORDAN'S BABY

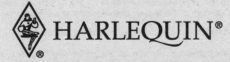

TORONTO • NEW YORK • LONDON
AMSTERDAM • PARIS • SYDNEY • HAMBURG
STOCKHOLM • ATHENS • TOKYO • MILAN • MADRID
PRAGUE • WARSAW • BUDAPEST • AUCKLAND

ISBN-13: 978-0-373-12557-9
ISBN-10:   0-373-12557-7

JACK RIORDAN'S BABY

First North American Publication 2006.

Copyright © 2006 by Anne Mather.

www.eHarlequin.com

Printed in U.S.A.

All about the author...
Anne Mather

I've always wanted to write—which is not to say I've always wanted to be a professional writer. For years I wrote only for my own pleasure and it wasn't until my husband suggested that I ought to send one of my stories to a publisher that we put several publishers' names into a hat and pulled one out. The rest, as they say, is history. And now, more than 150 books later, I'm literally—excuse the pun—staggered by what happened.

I had written all through my childhood and into my teens, the stories changing from children's adventures to torrid Gypsy passions. My mother used to gather these up from time to time, when my bedroom became too untidy, and dispose of them! The trouble was, I never used to finish any of the stories, and *Caroline*, my first published book, was the first book I'd actually completed. I was newly married then, and my daughter was just a baby, and it was quite a job juggling my household chores and scribbling away in exercise books every chance I got. Not very professional, as you can see, but that's the way it was.

I now have two grown-up children, a son and daughter, and two adorable grandchildren, Abigail and Ben. My e-mail address is mystic-am@msn.com and I'd be happy to hear from any of my readers.

CHAPTER ONE

'THERE'S A YOUNG lady to see you, Mrs Riordan.'

The housekeeper had emerged through the long windows at the back of the house and now stood looking at Rachel as she finished clipping a long-stemmed white rose and laid it in a trug at her feet.

Rachel straightened. She was neither in the mood nor dressed for visitors. The woman couldn't be someone she knew or Mrs Grady would have said so. She had to be either one of Jack's clients or collecting for charity. In which case, why hadn't Mrs Grady dealt with it herself?

'Didn't you tell her that Mr Riordan's not here?' she asked, deciding it must be one of Jack's clients. How she'd got his address, heaven knew, but then, Jack rarely abided by any of the rules that she'd always been taught to obey.

'She doesn't want to see Mr Riordan,' said Mrs Grady at once. 'She asked to speak to you, Mrs Riordan. She says her name's Karen Johnson. She seemed to think you'd know who she was.'

All the blood seemed to drain out of Rachel's body at that moment. She felt both sick and dizzy. She might have lost her balance had it not been for the trellis close by that provided a convenient place to rest her trembling hand. But

Mrs Grady knew her too well not to notice her sudden pallor, and, hurrying across the terrazzo tiles of the patio, she took Rachel's arm in a reassuring grasp.

'There now,' she said reprovingly. 'I knew you shouldn't have been working out here in the hot sun without a hat. You've overdone it, haven't you? Come along inside and I'll get you a nice cool glass of iced tea.'

'I'm all right, really.' Rachel could feel faint colour coming back into her face as she spoke. 'Um—where is Miss—Miss Johnson? Perhaps you'd better show her into the drawing room while I go and wash my hands.'

'Now, is that wise?' Mrs Grady had picked up the trug of roses, and with the familiarity of long service she gave her mistress a doubtful stare. Then, retaining her hold on Rachel's arm, she urged her towards the house. 'I can easily tell the young lady you're not available. If it's important, I'm sure she can come back another day.'

Rachel was tempted. Unbearably tempted. But putting it off wasn't going to make it go away. All the same, she was stunned by the woman's nerve in coming here. Had Jack put her up to this? Somehow, despite his faults, Rachel doubted even *he* would be that cruel.

'Just show her into the drawing room, Mrs Grady,' she said now, firmly putting all thought of changing her mind aside. 'I won't be long. You can serve us both some iced tea in the meantime.' Though whether she would be able to swallow anything in Karen Johnson's presence was uncertain.

Rachel took the back stairs to the upper floor, entering her bedroom with some relief. Despite what she'd told Mrs Grady, she still felt a little unsteady, so she went into the adjoining bathroom and sluiced her hot face with cold water from the gold-plated taps.

The beauty of her surroundings went some way to calming her. This suite of rooms—sitting room, bedroom and bathroom—was hers and hers alone, and although it was more extravagant than she could have wished, she couldn't deny it soothed her frazzled nerves.

That *that* woman should have the audacity to come here, she thought incredulously. And then, hard on the heels of that thought, Why on earth had she come? What could they possibly have to say to one another? She was Jack's mistress; Rachel was Jack's wife. Surely anything she had to say should be said to him?

She stared at her reflection in the long mirror above the vanity. God, she looked as shocked as she felt. Like a rabbit caught in the headlights of an oncoming vehicle, she mused raggedly. With just as much sense of how to prevent the inevitable from happening.

But this wouldn't do. She couldn't let this woman come here and intimidate her in her own home. She was the mistress here, not Karen Johnson. If she had any sense she'd send the woman packing without even hearing what she had to say.

But it was too late to be thinking that. Already Karen Johnson was in her drawing room, being served iced tea by her reluctant but unfailingly polite housekeeper. She couldn't keep her waiting. She *shouldn't* keep her waiting. She mustn't give the woman any reason to believe that she was too timid to confront her husband's whore.

Taking a deep breath, Rachel surveyed her appearance with a critical eye. It was a very warm day, and because she hadn't been expecting any visitors, she'd chosen to wear pale green linen shorts and an aqua silk top. The top was loose and sleeveless, exposing the faint reddening of sunburn on her arms.

Should she change? Should she put on some make-up before meeting her guest? Perhaps some eyeshadow, she decided, shading her lids from beige to umber. And a brown-tinted lip gloss to complement the sun-streaked colours in her blond hair.

Surveying her appearance once more, Rachel professed herself satisfied with the result. In any case, she'd taken long enough. She didn't want Karen thinking she'd dressed especially for her. Taking another deep breath, she glanced about the elegant room to give herself confidence. But she had the uneasy feeling that, whatever happened between her and this woman, nothing was ever going to be the same again.

Karen was seated on one of the trio of velvet sofas that flanked the fireplace in the drawing room. Another elegant apartment, the windows here were open to the garden at the back of the house. Although the place had an efficient air-conditioning system, Rachel much preferred fresh air. When she was alone in the house, as now, she invariably had all the windows open.

Rachel hesitated on the threshold, for once less than confident as a hostess. Karen looked so relaxed, so at home here, she thought tensely. A stranger might be forgiven for mistaking Rachel as the intruder and Karen as the mistress of the house.

Unlike Rachel, Karen was quite formally dressed, considering the heat of the day. A short-skirted pale pink suit exposed her legs and her cleavage and, although she didn't appear to be wearing any stockings, she had high-heeled pumps on her feet.

She looked—sure of herself, thought Rachel uneasily. Smart and sophisticated, confident in her ability to catch a man's eyes. She was also a redhead, Rachel noticed, although she doubted that was any more natural than the smile that spread over her full lips when she saw Rachel in the doorway.

She got to her feet at once and, despite Rachel's initial impressions, there was tension in the way she clutched her handbag with both hands. She wasn't as tall as Rachel, who was five feet ten even in her bare feet, but she was voluptuous, her heavy breasts almost spilling from a scarlet bustier.

She didn't immediately say anything, however. She just stood there, looking at Rachel, waiting for her to make the first move. Rachel wanted to shout, *What the hell are you doing in my house?* But that would have sounded childish. So, instead, she moved into the room and said with what she thought was admirable coolness, 'Miss Johnson, I presume?' as if she hadn't already seen pictures of her with Jack. 'If you're looking for my husband, I'm afraid he's not here.'

'I know that, Mrs Riordan.' The confidence was back, and if she'd been surprised that Rachel should recognise her so easily she managed to hide it. 'He's in Bristol, signing the contract for the new shopping development.'

So she knew his schedule, thought Rachel, striving for indifference. No doubt Jack kept her informed of his movements. 'You're right,' she said casually, although Jack rarely told her where he was going these days. 'Which makes me wonder why you'd come here, Miss Johnson. I don't think you and I have anything to say to one another.'

'Oh, we do.' Karen didn't wait for an invitation before subsiding onto the sofa again. 'Why don't you join me, Mrs Riordan? What I have to tell you may cause you some distress.'

Rachel wondered idly how much it would cost to replace all three of the sofas. Several thousand pounds—but it might be worth it not to have to remember this scene. 'I'll stand,' she said, hoping the other woman would take the hint and make this—whatever it was—brief. She had no desire to get cosy with her.

'As you please.'

Karen shrugged her shoulders, but before she could say anything more Mrs Grady bustled into the room with a tray containing two tall glasses and a jug of iced tea. Rachel remembered asking the housekeeper to provide the tea in the first few moments after learning Karen was here. Now she wished she hadn't, but it was too late to have second thoughts.

'There, now. Is there anything else I can get you, Mrs Riordan?' Mrs Grady asked, eyeing her with some concern.

'No, that's all.' Rachel managed a terse smile. 'Thank you.'

'Well, you sit down and take it easy,' advised the housekeeper shrewdly. 'You're still looking peaky. Are you sure you're feeling all—'

'I'm fine, Mrs Grady.' The last thing Rachel wanted was for Karen Johnson to think her arrival had caused her to feel ill. Or distressed, she added silently, giving the housekeeper a meaningful stare. 'If I want anything else, I'll let you know.'

Mrs Grady arched her brows, but she had the sense not to argue, and after she'd gone Rachel gestured towards the tray. 'Help yourself,' she said, refusing to put herself in the position of having to serve her. 'You must be hot,' she continued. 'I hope you didn't wear that suit for my benefit.'

She had the shabby pleasure of seeing how Karen bristled at this comment. But what the hell? Rachel thought defensively. She deserved worse than that for having the nerve to come here. What did she want, for God's sake? Wasn't the fact that she was sleeping with Jack enough for her? Did she have some notion of splitting them up as well?

'I always dress for the occasion,' Karen replied at last, having considered her argument. 'Clothes are so important, don't you think? Particularly if you want to please a man.'

'I dress to please myself,' retorted Rachel, not altogether truthfully. But she'd used to, she reminded herself staunchly. Before Jack Riordan had entered—and subsequently ruined—her life.

'I can see that,' Karen said now, leaning forward to pour herself a glass of the cool beverage Mrs Grady had provided. Ice chinked and Rachel wished she could pour one for herself. But she didn't trust her hand not to shake as she did so, and that would be a dead giveaway. No, better to remain where she was until the woman had gone.

'Mmm, delicious.' Whether she'd detected Rachel's ambivalence or not, Karen raised the glass to her lips and deliberately savoured her first mouthful. A pink tongue appeared to collect every drop from her glossy lower lip and she sighed with pleasure. 'Are you sure you won't change your mind, Mrs Riordan? I'm sure you must be feeling as hot as me.'

Rachel shifted to stand beside the sofa opposite. Then, resting one hand lightly on the soft cushion, she said calmly, 'I'll survive. Why don't you get to the point, Miss Johnson? If your intention was to shock me with your existence, then, as you can see, you're wasting your time.'

Karen set the glass back on the tray and folded her

hands together in her lap. Then she looked up at the other woman with malicious eyes. 'You think you're so secure, don't you, Rachel?' she mocked, obviously using her name to show she wasn't intimidated by her attitude. 'I wonder how you'll feel when I tell you I'm expecting Jack's baby?'

A pain sharper than a rapier seared through Rachel's stomach at her words. It took every ounce of will power she had not to cry out at the agony it caused. It couldn't be true, she told herself. The woman had to be lying. After all the misery she'd suffered trying to give Jack the child he wanted, surely he had more compassion than to make his mistress pregnant?

She became aware that Karen was watching her with a shrewd, assessing gaze, and despite what she'd been thinking she instinctively sensed that the other woman knew about her three miscarriages. Had Jack told her? He might have done. Though Rachel preferred to believe that someone in his office was responsible.

It wasn't a secret, for God's sake. In the beginning Jack had been only too eager to broadcast the fact that he was going to be a father to the world. It was only after she'd lost two babies a few weeks into the first trimester that he'd chosen to keep her next pregnancy a secret. Which was just as well, because she'd lost that baby, too.

But this wasn't the time to be having thoughts like these. With Karen's eyes on her face, watching for any sign of weakness, Rachel knew she had to hide her real feelings until after the woman was gone.

All the same, she couldn't help sinking down onto the arm of the sofa. Her legs were definitely not strong enough to support her at this moment, and she just hoped she didn't look as horrified as she felt.

She knew she was pale, but she couldn't help that. She

was probably as white as a sheet, but somehow she had to force her frozen features into speech.

Before she could say anything, however, Karen shifted forward in her seat and poured some of the iced tea into a second glass. 'Here,' she said, holding it out, but although the gesture seemed considerate enough Rachel knew there was no real sympathy in the act.

'No—thanks,' she muttered, almost choking on the word, and Karen shrugged before setting the glass down again.

'Suit yourself,' she said carelessly. Then, arching her dark brows, 'So—what are you going to do about it?'

Rachel stared at her in disbelief, realising she hadn't the first idea what to say. Questions like: *How many months are you*? and *Have you told Jack*? were totally beyond her. The truth was, she didn't want to know the answers. Obviously Karen's pregnancy had been confirmed or she wouldn't have come here. But surely if Jack had known about it he would have told her, *warned* her? Or perhaps not. Oh, God, she didn't think she could handle this.

Moistening her lips, she took the only course open to her. 'What am I going to do about it?' she echoed, amazed that her voice sounded so normal. 'I don't think I understand that question. I have no intention of doing *anything*, Miss Johnson. If you're pregnant—and I only have your word for that—then surely it's up to you to deal with it in whatever way you choose?'

'Oh, no.' Karen surged to her feet, anger thickening her voice. 'You're not going to get away with that, *Mrs* Riordan. I didn't come here to be dismissed like some charity case.'

The one-liner *Where do you usually go*? rose like hysteria in the back of Rachel's throat, but she fought it down.

This was no laughing matter, and not for the first time she wished her mother were still alive.

But she wasn't. She'd been dead for over ten years. No one could help her now except herself, and as Karen geared herself up for another offensive, she said firmly, 'I'm sorry you feel like that, Miss Johnson. But there's really nothing I can do.'

'Like hell!' Karen glared at her across the wide expanse of Persian carpet. 'You can start by giving Jack a divorce. Or are you so selfish you'd deprive him of the chance of ever having a son of his own?'

Rachel had thought there was nothing the woman could say now that would hurt her more than she'd been hurt already. But she'd been wrong.

'You must know he only married you to get control of your father's business,' Karen continued contemptuously. 'Women like you make me sick. All your life people have protected you, looked after you, made absolutely sure the little princess didn't get her hands dirty with anything remotely approaching work!'

'That's not true!'

Despite her determination not to get involved in an argument with this woman, Rachel had to defend herself. All right, when she'd married Jack she'd just left art college and she hadn't been looking for a job. But she had already been putting out feelers to publishers, offering her work for consideration, and by the time she'd found she was pregnant she'd been working on her first attempt at illustration.

In any case, it didn't matter, because Karen ignored her. 'I don't know why you married Jack,' she went on in the same disparaging tone. 'Or rather, I do. But, aside from the fact that he's drop-dead gorgeous, you must have known he didn't love you. I mean, he's a real man. Not one of the pretty public schoolboys you're used to.' She gave a smug little smile. 'Jack's not like that. He's not soft. And he needs a real woman. Me.'

'Really?'

Somehow Rachel managed to sound bored by her submission, and was pleased when it aroused an entirely different expression on Karen's face.

'Yes, really,' she snapped, her anger never far from the surface. 'That's why I've come to see you. Jack didn't want to hurt you. He feels sorry for you, I suppose. But the situation can't be allowed to continue. Not now that I'm going to have his baby.'

Rachel got to her feet. She still felt unsteady and strangely distant, as if this was some surreal happening she was just a witness to. But she couldn't allow her to go on. Not if she wanted to retain any semblance of self-respect. This was her house—and Jack's, but that was immaterial—and she couldn't let the woman make a victim of her in her own home.

'I think you'd better go, Miss Johnson,' she said now, and even Karen looked taken aback at the apparent authority in her tone. She crossed the room, albeit on rather stiff legs, and rang the bell for the housekeeper. 'Mrs Grady will show you out. Please don't come here again.'

Karen took an aggressive step towards her. 'You can't treat me like this.'

'Oh, I think I can.' Rachel's voice gained more confidence from her enemy's agitation. 'You're not welcome here, Miss Johnson. Be thankful I'm not calling the police to throw you out.'

'You wouldn't dare!' Karen stared at her hard, as if trying to ascertain whether she meant what she said. Then she gave a scornful laugh. 'Imagine what the gutter press would make of you hounding your husband's mistress. No, you're bluffing, Mrs Riordan. You're probably wetting your pants for fear I might go to the papers myself.'

'Get out!' Rachel's voice trembled as she spoke, but her determination didn't falter. As she was taller than Karen, she used her height to make her point. 'Get out before I throw you out,' she snarled, her hands balling into fists at her sides. And, although Karen retained her air of defiance, she moved reluctantly towards the door.

'You haven't heard the last of me,' she said provokingly, and Rachel wondered where Mrs Grady was when she needed her. 'Wait until I tell Jack how you've treated me. You won't be half so cocky then.'

'Oh, *I'm* the one who'll be telling Jack about your visit,' retorted Rachel recklessly. 'Yes, he's going to be delighted when he hears your opinion of his character.'

'What do you mean?'

Karen was wary, and Rachel gave her a mocking smile. 'I can't wait to tell him that you think he only married me to get control of the company. I mean, you're virtually saying he couldn't have made it on his own.'

'You cow!'

'Me?' Rachel was actually starting to enjoy herself in a disreputable way. 'What's the matter, Miss Johnson? Are you beginning to realise you might have said too much?'

'No.' But Karen was agitated. 'I don't care what you say, I'm going to have Jack's baby. You might earn a few points for effort, Mrs Riordan, but I'm holding the winning card.'

Rachel's nails dug into her palms, but before she could stop herself she said, 'One of them.' And, as Karen turned incredulous eyes in her direction, she added unforgivably, 'Didn't he tell you? I'm having a baby, too.'

CHAPTER TWO

IT WAS LATE when Jack got back to Market Abbas.

The actual signing of the contract hadn't taken long, but there'd been lunch with the Mayor, followed by a tour of the city, then drinks—something he always tried to avoid these days—before an early dinner with the architect, the surveyor, and other dignitaries. Jake knew they were only there for the ride, but he had to play along despite how he was feeling before he could reasonably take his leave.

It had all gone very well, and everyone had seemed satisfied with the deal. Jack felt he'd acquitted himself adequately considering he hadn't been in the mood for any of it. Since he'd spoken to his doctor on Tuesday he'd been having a hard time making sense of his life, let alone anything else.

It was just as well he and Rachel spent so little time in each other's company these days. In the early months of their marriage she'd have known instantly that something was wrong. These last few months had been hell. He was sleeping badly and his appetite was virtually non-existent. The pressure of work, of handling the continued expansion and the other responsibilities he had now that Rachel's father was dead, was crippling. And now dealing with Karen

Johnson as well had proved too much. Even Mrs Grady had noticed, but she knew better than to interfere.

Driving between the open gates of the house he'd built just after he and Rachel were married, Jack knew an overwhelming sense of relief. He was grateful for the darkness, too, to hide the weariness he knew must be evident in his face. After all, his home was over a hundred miles from Bristol, and, although he loved driving, he wished he'd let his driver take the wheel tonight.

But that would have meant Dan couldn't have had a drink either, and that wouldn't have been fair. And the last thing he wanted was for Dan to become suspicious of his health. He might feel it was his duty to inform Rachel. He had always been very fond of Jack's wife.

There were lights on in the house, even though it was after eleven o'clock. Someone must still be up, and he guessed it was Mrs Grady. The days when Rachel had waited up for him were long gone. His expression shifted to one of regret. He missed those late-night conversations with his wife, the opportunities they'd given him to get the events of the day into perspective. They hardly discussed the company these days. And since her father had died two years ago, he'd had no one in the family to share his problems with.

So whose fault was that?

But Jack had no desire to get into such things tonight. He was too tired, too depressed, too sick of being the boss of Fox Construction first and Jack Riordan second.

He sighed, and after parking the Aston Martin to one side of the entrance he got out of the car. He couldn't be bothered to put it in the garage. If it was stolen, so be it. He didn't much care either way.

His lips twisted. Life was like that. It gave you everything you'd ever want with one hand and took it back with the other. What was that word? *Schadenfreude*? Malicious pleasure at another's expense? Yeah, that was probably a good way to describe the way fate had treated him.

His cellphone chirped in his pocket and, stifling a curse, he pulled it out. Karen! As he'd expected. He pressed the disconnect button and severed the call. She'd been calling him off and on all day—hell, for the past three months— and he had no desire to speak with her tonight.

Turning the phone off, he used his key quietly, mindful that Rachel was probably asleep by now. She'd always been a light sleeper, waking as soon as he'd entered their bedroom. Not that they shared a bedroom these days. Since she'd lost the last baby Rachel had left him in no doubt that she preferred to sleep alone.

There were lamps glowing in the wide entrance hall, casting a mellow light across the parquet floor. Paintings that he and Rachel had chosen together were only shadows against the walls, and overhead the Waterford chandelier was dark.

Most of the downstairs rooms opened into the hall, but the doors were closed and no inviting ribbon of light showed beneath any of them. There appeared to be a light on the galleried landing, but he ignored it. If Mrs Grady was still up, she'd be in the kitchen, and Jack walked through the doorway behind the stairs that gave access to the housekeeper's domain.

To his surprise, the kitchen was dark as well. When he flicked a switch concealed lighting flooded granite surfaces and pale oak units but the room was empty. Scowling, he crossed to the double fridge and freezer, opening the fridge door and taking out a carton of milk. He glanced round for a glass, but that was too much trouble as well, so instead he raised the carton to his lips.

He took a healthy gulp, savouring its richness, wiping the smear from his upper lip with the back of his hand. The milk was cold and refreshing and, closing the fridge again, he took the carton with him when he left the kitchen to make his way upstairs.

It would probably do him more good than the fillet steak he'd only picked at earlier, he reflected, loosening his tie with his free hand. And Mrs Grady could hardly complain when she was always telling him he ought to have a more nutritious diet.

But he forgot all about the housekeeper as he neared the first floor landing. He was gradually realising there was too much light up here than could be accounted for by the courtesy light Rachel usually left burning. There was heat, and a curious smell of—what? Perfume? Incense? And a strange flickering incandescence coming through the open doors of Rachel's room.

The first thing that occurred to him was fire. He could think of no other reason for the flickering light. His heart-rate quickened and he tried not very successfully to calm himself. Oh, God, surely none of the calls he'd ignored had been from here?

Dropping the thankfully almost empty carton, he sprinted across the landing. Despite his protests, Rachel had moved out of the master suite and now occupied one of the four guest suites on the opposite side of the house. He couldn't think of any other reason why her doors should be open, and, although there was an increasing tightness in his chest, he was more concerned about his wife than about his own health.

The sight that met his eyes almost took his breath away altogether. There was fire all right, and flames, but they came from dozens of scented candles set all around the bedroom. There were tall ones, thin ones, squat ones, and some that didn't fit any particular pattern, and the heat and the scent were dizzying in their potency.

He halted in the doorway, one hand pressed to his madly beating heart, the other supporting himself against the jamb. He could see through a breathless haze that the bed was turned down, but the room was empty. As if some force had spirited Rachel away and left these burning symbols in her place.

He fought for breath, resting his full weight against the doorpost now, trying to make sense of what he was seeing. What did it mean? Was Rachel into some weird religious ritual or something? Why else would she have lit all these candles. Dear God, what was going on?

Fumbling in the inside pocket of his jacket, he found the strip of foil-wrapped pills the doctor had given him. Releasing one, he stuffed it in his mouth, feeling some relief as his heartbeat began to slow. Maybe Rachel knew about his condition and was trying to kill him, he thought, a faint smile appearing at the obvious irony. But what the hell? He'd be unwise to subject himself to too many shocks like this.

He was attempting to straighten up when the door to Rachel's bathroom opened. As he stared in disbelief, she stepped, barefoot, into the room. In the light from the scented candles he saw her eyes dart in his direction. But then his gaze was riveted by the fact that she was practically nude.

But 'nude' was a relative word, he acknowledged, aware that sometimes the anticipation was more satisfying than the reality. Though not in this case. In a black lace half-bra that gave her small breasts a surprising cleavage, and the minutest black lace thong he'd ever seen, she was stunning. A slim, long-legged goddess, whose scant underwear revealed that her mane of sun-streaked blond hair was most definitely natural.

'My God!'

The breathless oath was uncontrollable, and Rachel turned innocent eyes in his direction. 'Oh, Jack,' she said softly, as if she'd only just noticed him. 'I've been waiting for you.'

Jack felt as though he must have died and gone to heaven. That mad sprint across the landing must have done it for him, and he was presently enjoying some fantasy life elsewhere. There was no way that what he was seeing was real. It was a dream. It had to be. A tantalising glimpse of how their lives could have been.

'Hi,' he said weakly.

It took an effort to get his tongue round the word. There were any number of things he wanted to say, he *ought* to say, but he was too bemused to be original.

'You look tired,' she said, seeming to float towards him across the thick white carpet that covered the floor. She halted in front of him, reaching up to push his unruly dark hair off his forehead. 'Has it been a stressful day?'

Her fingers were cool against his hot forehead, and when she stretched the skimpy bra exposed a half-circle of the rosy flesh surrounding her nipple. She didn't seem to notice, but he did. The heated scent of her body was more potent than the candles that surrounded her.

Jack felt his body hardening instantly. It might be more than two years since he and Rachel had made love, but he remembered how incredible the sex between them used to be. Unfortunately, he'd only had to touch her for her to get pregnant, and time—and painful experience—had taught him that she wouldn't welcome his lovemaking again.

'Rachel,' he said, hearing the hoarseness of his voice, feeling his heart quickening its beat in spite of the drug he'd swallowed.

'Come on, Jack,' she responded, taking his hand and drawing him into the warmth and light of the bedroom. She gestured towards the huge Colonial-style bed that they had never shared. 'Sit down. Would you like a drink?'

There was nothing Jack would have liked more, but he shook his head. If this were a dream he didn't need alcohol to stoke his libido, and if it weren't he shouldn't be drinking alcohol, period.

He let her bring him into the room, allowed her to close the doors behind them and push him down onto the side of the wide bed. The truth was, his legs felt a little unsteady. But it was as much from the arousal she was generating as from the latent effects of his condition.

He caught his breath when she knelt down in front of him. What now? he thought, wondering if a man could die from illusions created by his own imagination. But all she did was remove his shoes and roll his socks down over his ankles. Then, when he was barefoot, she slipped those soft hands beneath the cuffs of his trousers and gently massaged his calves.

She offered him a demure smile when he rested back on his elbows, his damp palms pressed into the coverlet for support. Did she know it was the only way he could stop himself from reaching for her? She had to be aware of his erection. Dammit, it wasn't something he could disguise, after all.

But all she said was, 'There—doesn't that feel better?' as if her sensuous ministrations were something he was used to. She couldn't be that ingenuous, he thought, so what in God's name was she playing at? The pain in his groin had convinced him that, however unlikely it seemed, this was really happening.

Nevertheless, when she got to her feet again, putting his eyes on a level with the black strings that tied the thong at her hips, he couldn't look away. His eyes were irresistibly drawn to the cluster of blond curls that were visible through the black lace, and he couldn't deny she was sexy as hell.

'Relax,' she said now, coming closer and reaching for his tie, which he'd partly loosened as he came upstairs. Slender fingers dealt with the knot, and if Jack hadn't been so conscious of her hip against his thigh he'd have admired her expertise.

As it was, he thought that relaxing was totally beyond his current capabilities. Which wasn't helped when she lifted one leg to kneel on the bed beside him and started unbuttoning his shirt. Her fingertips brushed his skin, her nails scraping sensually over the fine dark hair that arrowed down to his navel and beyond. She was steadily driving him crazy and he had to stop her.

'Rachel,' he protested weakly, but when he lifted his hand he lost his balance and his back hit the mattress with a distinct thud. Then, to his amazement, she climbed totally onto the bed and threw one leg across him, straddling him as she continued to unfasten his shirt and pull it free of his pants.

The knowledge that her spread thighs were pressing down onto his groin almost overwhelmed him. He'd never been so close to losing control, and he closed his eyes to shut out the incredible sight of her leaning over him, her luscious breasts only inches from his mouth.

He felt her push his shirt and jacket over his shoulders, and then she turned her attention to the buckle on his belt.

He knew he ought to stop her. He *wanted* to stop her, he told himself. But his hands wouldn't obey what his brain was telling them. Instead, he let her loosen his pants and draw the zip down partway.

'Mmm,' she murmured, and he knew she must have discovered that his boxers were no barrier to the heavy thrust of his shaft. But, although he'd expected her to stop then, she only drew the blue silk aside and took him into her hands.

'Rachel,' he muttered, his eyes opening to find her bending to caress him with her tongue. 'What do you think I'm made of?'

Rachel lifted her head, her smile strangely triumphant. 'Oh, I know what you're made of,' she said, her tongue appearing again, to circle her lower lip with seductive deliberation. 'Flesh and sinew and—' she stroked a finger along his length '—blood and bone. Exactly what a man should be made of, don't you agree?'

Jake expelled a tortured breath. 'What do you think you're doing?'

Rachel arched brows that were several shades darker than her hair while eyes as deep a blue as indigo assessed him with disturbingly intensity. 'I thought I was helping you to undress,' she replied with artless innocence, and Jack swore.

'Have you been drinking?'

'Mmm.' She nodded eagerly. 'I had some tea earlier. Iced tea. Would you like some?'

Jack stared at her disbelievingly. 'Are you for real?'

'I hope so.' She straightened her spine, so that her weight was lifted off him, and ran exploring hands down her body from her breasts to her hips. 'I think so.' She paused. 'Don't you think I am?'

Jack didn't know what to think. 'Is this some sick game

you're playing?' he demanded harshly. 'Because I have to tell you, if it is, I—'

'It's no game, Jack.' Rachel looked positively offended now, and as he watched with incredulous eyes she swung herself off him and started to crawl towards the edge of the bed. 'I just thought we might—connect. You know? But—if you don't want to…'

'Want to?' Jack echoed her words with a feeling of frustration that knew no bounds. 'God, Rachel, of course I want to.' He pushed himself up, tearing off the shirt and jacket that were restricting his arms and tossing them on the floor. He restored himself to some semblance of modesty and scrambled after her, only his hipbones and good fortune keeping his pants from slipping down his thighs. 'For pity's sake, come here!'

With his heart pounding so heavily against his ribcage that he was afraid it was going to burst out of his chest, he managed to snag her ankle, preventing her from climbing off the bed. And although he'd expected her to object she didn't. She let him pull her towards him, twisting obediently onto her back and provocatively spreading her legs.

'Is this better?' she asked huskily, and Jack could only gaze at her with stunned disbelieving eyes.

He expelled a harsh breath, still not entirely convinced she meant what she said. His stomach was twisted as tight as a drum, and although his senses were telling him to take what she was offering without further explanation, a latent instinct for self-preservation warned him that nothing was ever that simple.

'Rachel,' he said, his voice uncertain even to his own ears. But she didn't want to talk.

Lifting her hand, she laid a slender finger across his mouth, and he couldn't stop his lips from turning against her soft skin. Capturing her hand, he brought her palm to his mouth, his tongue seeking the texture and the taste of her. But before he could do more than touch her she snatched her hand away.

'I thought you wanted me,' she whispered, reaching for his belt and using it to tantalise him. 'But you're vastly overdressed.'

Jack could hardly breathe. Whatever way he wanted to play it, this was like some crazy dream, and he was no longer capable of dividing the illusory from the reality. Somehow he managed to push his suit pants and his boxers down his legs, kicking them off the bed, too. Then he knelt beside her, content for a moment just to marvel at his own good luck.

She was beautiful, he thought unsteadily. He'd almost forgotten how incredibly beautiful she was. Small, high breasts, a narrow waist, and hips that flared sweetly above long, sexy legs. Her skin was smooth, unblemished, honey-toned from the hours she spent outdoors. The Devon coast could be as hot as the Mediterranean, and Rachel had always loved the sun.

He allowed his hand to skim the slopes of her breasts above the provocative line of the bra. Then, with a little less restraint, he dipped his hand into the lace and cupped one warm rounded globe.

Her nipple was hard. It thrust against his palm. He didn't need to glance at himself to know that his erection was hard and prominent, too. It jutted from its soft nest of dark hair with a total lack of modesty.

'You're overdressed, too,' he said thickly, unable to re-sist tugging on the strings that tied the thong and pulling it away. 'That's much better.'

She shifted a little restlessly when he replaced the thong

with his hand, his thumb finding the throbbing nub of her womanhood, his fingers discovering that she was wet and ready for him.

And, God, he was ready for her, he thought, stretching beside her and seeking her moist mouth with his lips. She was all he wanted, had ever wanted before three miscarriages and her refusal to let him near her had got in the way.

He was sorry when she turned her head to one side, preventing him from prolonging the kiss. Apparently Rachel wasn't interested in foreplay. Or else, like himself, she was eager to consummate their reunion. There was no denying he couldn't wait to be a part of her again. Even his wildly beating heart couldn't deter him.

Her bra had a front fastening; so convenient, he thought gratefully, releasing it easily. Her breasts spilled into his hands, but when he would have taken one swollen nipple into his mouth she shook her head.

'Please, Jack,' she said, taking his face between her palms. 'Just—do it.'

Jack was more than willing. But after he'd moved to kneel between her spread thighs he remembered he had no protection. 'I—I don't have a—'

He gestured meaningfully, but Rachel didn't seem concerned. 'It's all right,' she whispered huskily, arching her body towards him in a tantalising invitation he couldn't resist. 'For pity's sake, Jack—'

He needed no second bidding. And, despite the fact that it had been more than two years since he and Rachel had last made love, they fitted together perfectly. He slid into her in one smooth, easy motion. Her tight muscles closed about him hotly, slickly, and Jack's head swam with the undiluted pleasure of it all.

'Oh, baby,' he breathed, burying his face in the scented

hollow between her breasts, and although until then she hadn't put her arms around him, now they came almost convulsively about his shoulders, holding him against her.

For a short while he was content to lie there with her, to feel the intimacy of man against woman, skin against skin. He felt himself stretching her and filling her, and his racing pulse gradually slowed its mindless beat.

But Rachel was restless, shifting beneath him, urging him to take what she'd so generously offered. So he began to move, slowly at first, withdrawing almost to the point of separation before sliding into her again.

He felt the sweat beading on his forehead, felt the restraint he was putting on himself tighten almost to breaking point. She was so desirable, so willing, and the fear that somehow, some way, this was going to be denied him, drove him to quicken his pace.

Yet there was no way this wasn't a benediction. He loved her sinuously, sensuously, arousing her almost in spite of herself, crazy as that seemed. But she wrapped one leg and then the other about his hips and he knew she couldn't control what was happening any more than he could.

He felt her muscles tighten about him only a moment before her climax shook her slender frame. He thought she might have cried out, though she stifled the sound against his chest. And Jack found his own release only seconds later, the rippling waves of her orgasm a potent stimulus he couldn't deny. For the first time in years, he spilled his seed inside her, feeling the shuddering warmth draining out of him, draining him, so that although he knew he must be crushing her, he didn't have the strength to roll away...

CHAPTER THREE

RACHEL WAS IN the kitchen with Mrs Grady when Jack came downstairs the next morning.

He'd wakened to find himself alone in the big bed and, judging by the fact that the other side of the mattress had been stone-cold, he suspected his wife had slept somewhere else. Someone, probably Rachel, had thrown the coverlet over his lower limbs—in deference to Mrs Grady's sensibilities, no doubt. But the candles had all guttered out, and, like any venue after a party, the room had felt stale and lifeless.

He'd thrown all the windows open before taking his shower, determined not to read too much into Rachel's absence. Then, because he wasn't planning on going into the office today, he'd dressed in a black tee shirt and his oldest pair of jeans. The jeans were tight, and worn in obvious places, so he left the button at his waist unfastened. He knew he felt better than he'd done for months—relaxed and rested. An unfamiliar condition for him these days.

Rachel was standing with her back against one of the limed oak units, a mug of what he guessed was coffee in her hand, talking to Mrs Grady. Unlike him, she didn't look either relaxed or rested, though Jack thought she could never look less than stunning. In a rose-patterned see-through voile shirt that tied at her waist, worn over an ivory vest and loose taupe trousers, she looked cool and elegant. Her straight blond hair was loose and brushing her collar, and his first thought was how sensuous it had felt against his skin the night before.

His entrance silenced the two women, however, but Jack refused to be deterred. 'Good morning,' he said into the sudden vacuum. 'Am I interrupting something?'

'Of course not, Mr Riordan.' It was Mrs Grady who answered, and Jack noticed Rachel avoided his eyes. 'I expect you'll be wanting breakfast. What can I get you?'

Jack wished Rachel would look at him, but after a brief glance in his direction she left him to speak to the housekeeper and went to stand in front of the huge porcelain sink, staring out at the garden at the side of the house. It wasn't unusual for her to ignore him. God knew, he'd gotten used to it over the past couple of years. But after last night he didn't understand her attitude, and as Mrs Grady busied herself taking eggs from the fridge, Jack crossed the room to stand beside his wife.

'Hi,' he said, his voice dangerously husky. 'I missed you when I woke up.'

Rachel took a sip of her coffee before replying. Then, 'Did you?' she said, without looking at him. 'I suppose you're used to sex in the morning as well.'

Now, why had she said that? As Jack stared at her with narrowed eyes, Rachel cursed herself for allowing her own inadequacies to colour her speech. For God's sake, the last thing she wanted was to think about sex with Jack. Or say anything to remind her of how perfect their lovemaking had been the night before.

It was hard enough just looking at him. Jack had always

been a good-looking man—'drop-dead gorgeous' was
what Karen had said—and even with a night's growth of
stubble on his chin Rachel had to agree with her. She as-
sumed he had his Irish heritage to thank for his dark hair,
which was usually too long and often unruly, and for his
green eyes, as pure and clear as a mountain lake—what
irony! And his strong, sensual features, which were too
hard-boned to be really handsome.

The whole added up to a man with a tenacity of purpose even her father had admired. The fact that he was also
tall and lean and moved with the sinuous grace of a big cat
gave him the kind of sexuality few women could resist.

The miracle was that he'd married her. They'd fallen in
love and theirs had been a fairy-tale romance. Rachel had
believed that nothing and no one could come between
them. But she'd been so wrong.

'Did I miss something?'

Jack's voice had an edge to it now that Rachel couldn't
mistake. She had to tell him, she thought. It wasn't fair to
let him go on thinking they were together again. But the
temptation was there to put it off for the time being. She
knew she'd need only to say the word for them to spend
the rest of the day in bed.

But she couldn't do that. Jack was like a drug, and it had
been hard enough to wean herself off him the first time
around. 'I'm sure you know what I mean,' she said, deliberately casual. 'I know you've been sleeping with—with other
women, Jack. You haven't lived like a monk all these months.'

'My God!' Jack's reaction was predictably violent and
Rachel cast an anxious look over her shoulder to see if Mrs
Grady was listening. But the housekeeper had left the
room, evidently deciding to leave them to it. 'Where the
hell did that come from?'

Rachel's mouth was dry. 'Well, it's the truth, isn't it? You have been seeing someone else?'

'I've seen a lot of people,' retorted Jack harshly. 'What's this all about, Rachel? What was last night all about? Why didn't you tell me how you felt before you—?'

He broke off abruptly, turning away to rake unsteady fingers through his hair. All of a sudden he felt sick and dizzy; the aftermath of too much excitement? he thought bitterly. Or anticipation of the nightmare to come?

'Jack?'

Rachel sounded almost concerned now, and he wondered if she'd guessed that something was wrong. But the last thing he needed was for her to feel sorry for him. He had some pride, albeit somewhat shredded after last night.

'Just go away, Rachel,' he said, gripping the overhanging lip of granite with both hands. He made a sudden decision. 'I've got to go into the office.' He straightened. 'I'll see you when I see you, right?'

Rachel touched his arm and he flinched. God, he had it bad, he thought. She'd only to lay a hand on him and he wanted to turn round and drag her—kicking and screaming, if necessary—into his arms. Despite his shaky equilibrium, and the fact that she'd apparently only been using him the night before, he still wanted her. And how pathetic was that?

'You're not dressed for the office,' she said now, and Jack knew he had to turn and face her.

'I was hungry,' he said, even though the thought of the omelette Mrs Grady had offered to make for him was making him feel sick.

Rachel's lips tightened. 'I suppose you can't wait to see her, can you?' she said, and Jack blinked at the sudden attack.

'To see *her?*' he echoed. 'Who the hell are you talking about?'

'This woman,' she persisted. 'She works in your office, doesn't she?' She paused, and when he made no reaction she went on, 'Karen Johnson? Don't pretend you've forgotten her.'

Jack swayed back on the heels of his loafers. 'How the hell do you know about her?'

'I know.' Rachel refused to tell him the woman had been here.

'I can't believe you were interested enough to investigate my life.'

'Can't you?' His words pained her, but she managed to hide it. 'I guess we don't know one another very well anymore.'

'And whose fault is that?' he countered, feeling his heart quickening in tune with his rising agitation. 'For God's sake, Rachel, *I* didn't move out of *your* bed!'

'You know why I did,' she cried, stung into defending herself, but Jack wasn't in the mood for compromise.

'They were my babies, too,' he said savagely. And then, feeling as if he'd pass out if he didn't get some air, he walked unsteadily across the kitchen floor. 'Just go to hell, Rachel,' he muttered, going out of the door.

Jack was sitting in his office in Plymouth, slumped over his desk, when the intercom buzzed. Scowling, he pushed himself up and pressed the answering button. 'Yeah?'

'You've got a call, Mr Riordan.' His secretary sounded apologetic. 'I know you said you didn't want to be disturbed, but it's your wife.'

'My wife?' Jack was stunned. He had no idea why Rachel should be ringing him after their altercation that morning. But he was ever the optimist, he thought dourly. 'Put her on.'

'Yes, Mr Riordan.'

The line went dead for a moment, and then a voice said, 'Hello, Jack.'

It wasn't Rachel. That was his first thought, and his spirits foundered. And because of that his response was savagely blunt. 'Karen,' he said, recognising her voice instantly after what Rachel had said. The way he was feeling now, if the woman had been in the immediate vicinity he'd have wrung her neck.

'Darling—you remember me!' she exclaimed, and Jack wondered how she expected him to forget. She'd been ringing him off and on for the past three months—ever since she'd been fired, actually. So many times, in fact, that he'd had to ask his secretary to monitor all his calls.

'Don't call me darling,' he snapped, wondering why he didn't just slam down the receiver. He'd done it before. 'Do you want to tell me what you're doing? Impersonating someone else is a criminal offence. If you ring this number again I'll have you arrested. There's a word for what you're doing, Karen, and it's harassment.'

'Oh, Jack, don't be so stuffy. You didn't used to be like this when we were together.'

'We were never together, Karen.' Jack was wearily aware he'd said all this before. 'We went out together once. And believe me, that was a mistake.'

Karen only laughed. 'You don't mean that, Jack.'

'Yes, I do. And I mean it when I say I'm going to report you to the authorities. I should have done it before. But I guess I felt sorry for you.'

'Don't feel sorry for me, Jack.'

Her tone had altered now, and he could tell he'd annoyed her. Well, good! Way to go. He hoped she'd got the message at last.

'Feel sorry for yourself, Jack,' she went on sharply. And then, her tone softening again, 'We need to be together. You know that. You can fight it if you like, but it won't do you any good.'

'For God's sake!' Jack lost patience. 'Get a life, Karen. One that doesn't include stalking me!'

He would have slammed the phone down then, but she must have sensed it, and rushed into speech. 'We're going to have a baby, Jack,' she burst out wildly. 'That's why I've been ringing you. We have to talk.'

Rachel spent the morning in the studio Jack had had built for her in the garden. It was on the far side of the property, with a magnificent view of Foliot Cove. The cove was at the foot of the cliffs that etched this part of the coastline, and could be reached by a flight of stone steps some previous owner of the land had had carved out of the rock.

Rachel was quite a gifted painter, using both oils and charcoal in various forms. But her favourite medium was watercolour, and she'd created quite a name for herself in recent years, illustrating children's books for the London publisher who'd recognised her talent.

Today, however, it was hard to concentrate. She kept thinking about what she'd done the night before, and remembering Jack's face when she'd told him she knew about his affair with Karen Johnson.

He hadn't admitted he was having an affair with Karen, but then he hadn't denied it either. Instead, he'd accused her of abandoning their marriage. Of moving out of their bed and effectively putting an end to their relationship.

Yet surely he should be able to understand how she'd been feeling at that time? Three times she'd become pregnant, three times she'd felt the miracle of life inside her, and three times she'd lost the baby in the third month. All right, perhaps she hadn't given enough thought to how Jack was feeling. Perhaps she had been totally tied up with her own emotions, her own grief.

But Jack had always seemed so strong, so impervious to anything life threw at him. The eldest son of an Irish labourer and his wife, who had emigrated to England in the sixties, he'd worked hard to get his degree in civil engineering. He was the only member of his family who'd ever gone to university, and although one of his brothers and all three sisters were settled now, with families of their own, for years Jack had helped to support his siblings, doing two jobs even when he was at university so that he could send money home.

She couldn't help wondering now if she'd been too quick to put his behaviour down to disappointment. Disappointment that he wasn't going to be a father, and disappointment in her, too, as a woman. She'd believed he thought she'd let him down—not once, but three times. And when she had refused to let him near her again, he'd turned to someone else.

It had all seemed so simple—and so sordid. She hadn't been able to believe that a man like Jack could exist without some woman in his bed. The fact that it had taken her almost eighteen months before she found out about his involvement with Karen Johnson didn't reassure her. Karen wasn't the first, she was sure. But she was the only one who'd got pregnant with his child.

At lunchtime, Rachel abandoned any attempt to continue with her painting of Benjie Beaver and went back to the house. She had still to explain to Mrs Grady why her bedroom had been littered with burnt-out candles that morning, and why Jack's bed hadn't been slept in.

However, Mrs Grady was out. She usually went shopping on Thursday mornings, Rachel remembered, finding even normal events as difficult to concentrate on as anything else. Karen Johnson's visit the day before—and her own shameless behaviour—had left her in a state of confusion. She knew that she'd seduced her husband. She just didn't know why.

Oh, there was the obvious reason: she wanted to get pregnant. But where was the sense in that? Why should she believe that this pregnancy—if indeed there was to be one—would be different from any of the others? Wasn't she just building up a whole lot of heartache for herself?

She shook her head. She only knew she'd had to do something to stop that woman from stealing her husband. Despite everything, she still loved him—although she had no intention of telling him that. But if she *was* expecting his child it would prove to Karen that they were sleeping together. And it gave her an added advantage. After all, she was still his wife.

To her surprise, Mrs Grady had left a cold lunch for two in the morning room. Chilled asparagus soup, a Caesar salad—Rachel's favourite—and strawberry shortcake for dessert. Rachel wondered if the housekeeper expected her to ask Lucy to join her. Her best friend, Lucy Robards, only lived half a mile away.

Rachel hadn't mentioned having a guest, so that seemed unlikely. But Jack never came home for lunch these days. It was a stretch if she had his company for dinner. Which was just as well, because they rarely had anything to say to one another.

An uncorked bottle of wine was standing in a cooler, and Rachel picked it out and poured some into a long-stemmed crystal glass. It was Chablis, she noticed as she tasted it. A wine that Jack had chosen. Was that relevant? Had he told Mrs Grady he'd be back for lunch?

It seemed unlikely. After the way he'd left the house earlier she was fairly sure she wouldn't see him again that day. But that wasn't entirely Jack's fault. She was going to bed earlier and earlier these days, escaping into oblivion to avoid the inevitable questions Jack's absence always created.

The roar of a car's engine in the drive caused a sudden quiver in her stomach. It could be Mrs Grady, of course, but she didn't think it was. Mrs Grady drove a Ford, not an Aston Martin. And this definitely sounded like a powerful car.

Rachel's nerves tightened instinctively, and she took a gulp of wine to calm her racing pulse. There was no reason to get all chewed up, she told herself. Jack had probably forgotten something. He'd probably come in and go out again without her even seeing him.

A car door slammed, and in spite of her assurances Rachel's mouth felt dry. She took another sip of wine, just to irrigate her throat, and then almost choked when Jack appeared in the open doorway.

She should have shut the door, she chided herself, still convinced he wasn't staying. But Jack had other ideas.

'Hi,' he said civilly, much to her surprise after the way he'd left the house. 'Good. I'm just in time.'

Rachel swallowed. 'This—' She gestured towards the round table, with its green and yellow place mats, its Villeroy and Boch china, its silver cutlery. 'This is for you?'

'For both of us,' amended Jack, taking off his charcoal suit jacket and dropping it over the back of one of the ladder-backed dining chairs. He loosened the top button of his shirt and pulled the knot of his silver-grey tie away from his collar. Then he approached the wine cooler where Rachel was standing, her wine glass forgotten in her hand. 'Is that Chablis?'

'Don't you know?' She couldn't keep the resentment out of her voice. 'I imagine you must have arranged this with Mrs Grady before you left.'

'I phoned,' he corrected her again, a flicker of his eyes registering the way she moved around the table to put some space between them. He helped himself to a little of the wine. But only a little, she noticed. Whatever else he'd come home for, it wasn't to drown his sorrows. He took a mouthful. 'Mmm, that's pretty good.'

Rachel shook her head, putting her glass down on the table with a slightly unsteady hand. She mustn't let him do this to her, she told herself. She wasn't going to let him behave as if nothing had happened. They both knew it had. Karen Johnson was part of their lives, for better or for worse.

All the same, as Jack stood there regarding her from beneath lashes any woman would have died for, Rachel was unwillingly reminded of the concern she'd had about him earlier. There was something different about him today. She didn't know what it was, but it troubled her.

'Shall we sit down?'

Jack spoke, and in spite of her thoughts Rachel gave a careless shrug. 'If you like.'

Jack waited until she'd taken the chair opposite before joining her. He wondered if she thought he hadn't noticed her edging her place setting around the table so that there was no way their elbows would touch, but he didn't comment on it. It was enough that she wasn't sniping at him—yet, anyway. No doubt that would come when he told her about Karen's call.

Rachel reached for the wine and refilled her glass. She felt as if she needed some false courage, and one glass just wasn't doing it. Despite her determination not to do so, she couldn't help wondering why there were those lines of strain beside his mouth. However strenuous last night had been—and she coloured at the memory—he had been as eager to satisfy his needs as she had been.

Realising he was waiting for her to have some soup before helping himself, Rachel lifted the lid of the tureen and ladled a spoonful into her bowl. Then she pushed the handle of the ladle in Jack's direction.

Judging by the little he took for himself, his appetite was as non-existent as her own, and once again she fretted over the reasons why. Last night he'd seemed exactly the same as usual; but then, last night she'd been intent on achieving her own ends, not his, she assured herself grimly.

Of course, his haggard appearance might have something to do with his guilty conscience, she thought, dipping her spoon into the soup with more force than enthusiasm. He was thirty-seven, for God's sake. What else could it be?

'Did you sleep well?'

His words took her completely by surprise—as they'd been meant to do, she guessed, annoyed that she'd been caught out. 'Not very,' she said, not altogether truthfully. After she'd left him sleeping soundly in her bed, she'd crashed in one of the other guest rooms. She must have been exhausted, because she hadn't been aware of anything until the morning sun had poured in through the uncurtained windows and she'd realised what she'd done. After that, sleep had definitely been out of the question.

Jack arched a disbelieving brow. 'Shame,' he said, putting his spoon aside. 'I slept like the dead.'

It was an unfortunate choice of words, particularly in

the circumstances, and Jack hoped they weren't prophetic. But Rachel was immune to their relevance.

'Now, why am I not surprised?' she asked scornfully. 'It comes of not having a conscience, I suppose.'

'I have a conscience.' Jack was stung into a retort. 'Do you?'

'Me?' Rachel was taken aback. 'Why should I have a conscience?'

'Well, let me see…' Jack lay back in his chair and toyed with his wine glass, but his eyes never left her flushed face. 'You don't think last night's play was just the tiniest bit unethical?'

Rachel moistened her dry lips. 'You're my husband. What was unethical about it?'

Jack let out a short laugh. 'Oh, baby, you don't really expect me to answer that?'

'Don't call me baby.'

'Why not?' Jack gave her an innocent look. 'Like you just said, I am your husband.'

Rachel pushed back her chair and got up from the table. 'If you'll excuse me—'

Jack got up, too, and blocked her exit. 'I won't,' he said, aware that he was probably blowing any chance of appealing to her better nature by acting this way, but he couldn't let her go like this. 'We're not finished yet.'

'I don't want anything more to eat.'

'I wasn't talking about the food.'

Rachel looked up at him with angry eyes. He guessed it was annoying her that in spite of her height he still had several inches on her. 'You can't keep me here.'

'Oh, I think I can.' Jack sidestepped—first one way, then the other, successfully preventing her from getting past him. 'Now, why don't you go and sit down again, and we'll talk?'

CHAPTER FOUR

'I DON'T WANT to talk to you.' Rachel was scowling now, and he could feel her frustration. The perfumed heat of her body was rising off her in waves, and after last night it was all he could do to keep a sense of perspective. 'And I don't want to sit down,' she added tersely. 'I want to go to my room.'

'Works for me.' Jack was willing. 'I'll come with you.'

'You won't!'

'No?' Jack adopted a puzzled look. 'It was okay for me to go there last night.'

'Last night was a mistake.'

'Right.' Jack pretended to consider it. 'So the whole scene: the absence of any electric lights, the incense-scented candles, you virtually naked, I'm to believe it was all a mistake?'

Rachel's chin dipped. 'Yes.'

'Why don't I believe you?'

She sniffed. 'Because you're too arrogant to think anything else?' she suggested, and he sighed.

'What are you saying? That it was for someone else?'

That thought had just occurred to him, and he didn't like it. But to his relief Rachel was too desperate to defend herself to lie.

'No,' she said fiercely. 'I don't sleep around.'

'Meaning I do?'

'If it fits.'

'It doesn't,' he snapped, momentarily angered by the unjust accusation. Then, calming himself, he went on, 'So it was all for my benefit?'

Rachel shifted uneasily. 'If you want to think that,' she muttered.

'What else am I supposed to think?' Jack lifted his hand, and in spite of her instinctive withdrawal he caught a strand of her silky hair and tucked it gently behind her ear. 'I didn't realise you were so needy.'

Rachel caught her breath. 'I'm not needy!'

Jack's fingers trailed from her ear down the smooth column of her throat to the low vee of her vest. 'You can't deny you wanted me last night.'

Rachel lifted her head. 'I—wanted a man, yes.'

Jack shook his head. He badly wanted to untie the shirt that hugged her midriff and slip his hands into the low waist of her trousers. But in spite of what she'd said he didn't think she'd let him do that, and he didn't want to destroy this tenuous relationship by rushing things. Instead, he contented himself with watching the way her nipples hardened against the fabric of her vest, remembering how delicious they'd felt rolling against his tongue.

'Look,' he said, after a moment, 'we have to talk about this. You can't expect me to ignore what happened and go on as before.'

'Why not?'

'Why not?' He stared at her frustratedly, his eyes darkening to the deepest shade of jade. 'Because it was good between us,' he said thickly. 'And I want to do it again.'

'No.'

Jack lifted his hand then, but although Rachel took an involuntary step back all he did was rake back his hair with an angry hand. 'So what now?' he demanded. 'Do I wait until the next time you feel like screwing me? Or do I get a say in the matter?'

Rachel's face burned. 'Don't use that word.'

'What word? Screwing? Well, that's what it was, wasn't it? I made love to you, but you screwed me!'

'No!'

'Yes.' Jack closed his eyes for a moment, striving for control. 'I should have known better than to think it was anything else.'

Rachel quivered. 'Well, what did you expect?'

Jack scowled. 'And that means *what*, exactly?'

Rachel took a deep breath. 'Haven't you forgotten Miss Johnson? What is she now, by the way? Your secretary? Your *personal* assistant? Oh, yes. Personal assistant just about covers it. She—'

'Karen doesn't work for the company any more,' he interrupted her.

Rachel stared at him disbelievingly. 'Since when?'

'Since George Thomas fired her.' Jack hadn't wanted to get into this right now, but he knew it was inevitable in the circumstances. 'What can I say? She was no good at her job. We had to let her go.'

'So how did she—'

Rachel had started to ask how Karen had known where Jack was and what he was doing, but then stopped herself. How silly was that? Just because the woman didn't work for Fox Construction any longer it didn't mean that Jack had stopped seeing her. He must think she was stupid if he thought that by telling her Karen had been dismissed she'd believe he'd ended their affair.

'How did she what?'

Jack had picked up on her unfinished question, and Rachel spent several unfruitful seconds trying to think of something else to ask.

'Um—how did she manage without a reference?' she asked at last. Then, seizing on his look of incredulity, 'Oh, right. You wrote one for her. What did you say, Jack? *Performs poorly in the office but makes up for it in bed*?'

'My God!' Jack groaned. 'You can't let it alone, can you? *You* don't want me, but you still think you have the right to control my life.'

Rachel flushed. 'No.'

'Yes.' Jack gave a harsh laugh. 'Tell me how that makes sense.'

'You don't understand—'

'Damn right.' Jack glared at her. 'Two years ago you let me know in no uncertain terms that you didn't want me anywhere near you. For weeks, months after that last miscarriage, you hardly even spoke to me.'

'I was traumatised!'

'So was I,' retorted Jack sharply. 'But I knew there was nothing I could about it.'

'You knew it wasn't your fault,' muttered Rachel, almost under her breath, but Jack heard.

'It was nobody's fault,' he snarled. 'For God's sake, I never blamed you, did I?'

'No...'

'So why the hell did you blame me? Because that's what it felt like. I was being punished because I couldn't keep my hands off you.'

'It wasn't like that.'

'So what was it like, Rachel?' He could feel himself getting stressed and, swinging out a chair from the table, he straddled it and sat down before he fell down. 'Tell me. Tell me why you've decided to stay married to me when you're obviously unhappy with the situation? For months we've been like strangers to one another—only speaking when we have to, only being seen out together when it's necessary to present a united front. If you want out, you should say so. Why the hell didn't you ask me for a divorce?'

'Why didn't you?'

'Me?' Jack blew out a heavy breath. 'I didn't want a divorce.'

'Why? Because you knew if you left me Daddy wouldn't make you his successor?'

'No!' Jack was stunned. It was one thing to be accused of having an affair; it was something else entirely to be suspected of being corrupt. 'For pity's sake, Rachel, where the hell did *that* come from? If you think I only married you to get my hands on your father's company—'

'I don't,' muttered Rachel in a small voice. And she didn't. Despite what she'd said, that particular aspect of Karen's argument still sounded alien even after what she'd learned. 'It was just something someone said.'

'What someone?'

Rachel hesitated, twisting the knot tying her shirt around her fingers. Then, with a rush of bravado, 'Karen Johnson.'

'What?'

Jack was amazed. He couldn't believe it. But, with the blood draining out of his brain, the dizziness he'd been having off and on for the past few weeks convinced him it was true. Somehow Rachel had been in touch with the other woman. But how, in God's name, had it happened?

'She—she came to see me,' Rachel went on doggedly, inadvertently answering the question he felt too numb to ask. She looked at him a little curiously. 'I gather you didn't know anything about it?'

'No.'

The word was clipped, and Jack shoved back his chair and got to his feet. Pacing somewhat unsteadily across the room, he managed to retain his balance. But he couldn't just sit there, blinking at her, knowing that sooner or later she was going to realise he was struggling for control.

Beyond the long windows, the Atlantic looked bluer than he'd ever seen it. White-capped waves curled in towards the beach, breaking on the rocks with a great swirl of spray. The ocean was so constant, he thought. Unlike people, it never changed. But the ocean was free, impartial. It didn't have a psycho like Karen making trouble in its life.

He glanced over his shoulder. Rachel still stood where he'd left her, her eyes flickering away when he found her watching him. What was she thinking? he wondered. That he was upset because he'd been found out?

'Are you saying she came here?' he asked, when he was capable of formulating a sentence, and Rachel gave a jerky nod.

'Yes.'

'When?'

Rachel looked discomforted now, and the reason for it occurred to him only seconds before she gave her answer.

'Yesterday,' she mumbled, turning back to the table and making an effort to gather their dirty dishes together. She cleared her throat. 'Are you going to have some salad?'

Jack's dizziness receded on a wave of disbelief. Anger gave strength to legs which only moments before had felt weak and uncertain. Striding back to the table, he caught her shoulder and swung her round to face him, uncaring of the look of apprehension in her eyes.

'Yesterday?' he exclaimed. 'Karen came here *yester-day*?' His heart was pounding in his chest but he ignored it. He hit his forehead with the palm of his hand. 'So *that's* what last night's little charade was all about!'

'Not necessarily.' Rachel pulled away from him. 'Anyway, you're my husband. Why shouldn't I sleep with you if I want to?'

Jack shook his head, unwilling to go into that right now. 'So go on,' he urged her harshly. 'What did she say?'

'Karen?'

'No, the cat's mother,' he snarled. 'Who else?'

Rachel straightened her spine. 'What do you think she said?'

Jack sucked in a frustrated breath. 'Don't do this, Rachel. I'm not in the mood to humour you.'

Rachel seemed to recover a little of her bravado. 'Oooh, I'm scared,' she mocked, only to break off with a gasp of pain when he manacled her wrist with hard, unyielding fingers. 'You're hurting me.'

'Believe me, this is nothing to what I'd like to do to you,' he told her harshly. 'Come on, Rachel. Spill!'

'Why don't you ask *her* if you're so interested?' she protested.

'Perhaps I will. But right now I'm asking you.'

Without warning, he took her wrist behind her back, jerking her towards him. Caught off balance, she couldn't prevent herself from reaching for him, her fingertips registering the heat beneath his shirt, the hard contours of his chest brushing the sudden arousal of her breasts.

God, for a moment she was stunned by her reaction, incapable of answering him for fear of showing how disturbed by his nearness she was. It convinced her that last night had been a massive mistake on her part. She'd stupidly believed she could seduce Jack without getting emotionally involved with him again, but she'd been wrong. Even though she'd avoided his kisses, knowing what his mouth could do to hers, already her body was betraying her, recognising his, responding to his, urging her to lean into him and give in to the wild abandonment of the senses she'd known the night before.

'Rachel!'

His harsh voice aroused her from the sensual pit she was digging for herself, and she tried to focus on what he'd asked her. But with his warm breath playing over her face and the male odour of his hot skin rising to fill her lungs with his scent, it was incredibly difficult to concentrate.

Definitely against her better judgement, her hand opened and her palm spread against his chest. She could feel his heart beating—thundering actually—against her fingers, and she guessed with a feeling of triumph that he was remembering last night, too.

'Jack…' she murmured, not really knowing what she was inviting, but unable to keep the yearning note out of her voice.

Jack swore. 'Don't go there, Rachel,' he warned, but already his eyes were dark with emotion, his lips only inches from hers.

He was going to kiss her, she thought, briefly blind to anything but her own needs. And why not? Why shouldn't she take what she wanted without considering the consequences? Other people did. Why shouldn't she?

'Rachel!'

Once again, Jack's saying her name brought an unwilling awareness of what she was doing, and she realised she'd been mistaken when she'd thought Jack was as aroused as she was. He was angry, that was all. Angry and frustrated. Well, she could play that game, too.

'Let go of me, Jack,' she said sharply, as if moments before she hadn't been practically begging for it. But Jack wasn't fooled.

'Not until you tell me what she said,' he grated. 'I want to know: did she tell you we were having an affair?'

Rachel heaved a sigh, giving in. 'You know she did,' she said wearily. 'But don't worry. It wasn't exactly news to me. I've known about your dirty little secret for some time.'

Jack stared down at her with disbelieving eyes. 'What do you mean, you knew?'

Rachel was tired of this. Grinding her heel into his toe, she got the advantage and pulled herself away from him 'I'm not a complete fool, Jack,' she said, as he winced in pain. 'You're not quite as clever as you thought you were.'

His eyes narrowed. 'And that means what, exactly?'

'The apartment you leased in Plymouth? The one you said you needed for entertaining clients? I know you take her there.'

Jack felt his stomach hollow. He *had* taken Karen to the riverside apartment, he remembered, but not to have sex with her. It had been while she was working for George Thomas. The company had just leased the furnished apartment, and Jack had needed someone to do an inventory of its contents for their records, and to make a note of what else was needed to make it habitable for clients.

George had offered Karen—mainly, Jack guessed, because it had been a job that she couldn't screw up. He'd driven her to the apartment himself, introduced her to the concierge so he'd know her presence was legitimate, showed her around and left. End of story.

It had been weeks later that he'd been foolish enough

to invite her to have dinner with him one evening when he was feeling low. He certainly hadn't taken her to the apartment on that occasion. But God knew what she'd told Rachel about it. Remembering what had happened that evening, he felt cold. He'd obviously given her the perfect opportunity to lie about it.

'I don't take anyone there,' he said now, knowing she wasn't going to believe him. 'The apartment is corporate property. Ask George Thomas if you don't believe me.'

'So you've never stayed there?'

Jack baulked. 'Okay, I've stayed there. On a couple of occasions. But I've been alone.'

Rachel shook her head. 'If you say so.'

'I *do* say so, dammit.' Jack could feel his head getting light and he struggled to keep himself grounded. 'For God's sake, Rachel, whatever that woman's told you, we have *not* been having an affair!'

'So how do you account for the fact that she's going to have your baby?'

Jack rocked back on his heels. 'What did you say?'

'I think you heard me.' Despite the accusation, Rachel couldn't quite meet his eyes, and once again she turned to the table and used the tongs to give the bowl of salad a quick turnover. Then, when the silence was beginning to scrape against her nerves, she went on jerkily, 'I really think you should eat something, Jack. Mrs Grady's gone to a lot of trouble, and she'll be so disappointed—'

'To hell with Mrs Grady!'

Jack had been standing staring at her for the last few minutes, watching as she made a play of checking the food. He was trying to remain calm, but his mind was racing quicker than his pulse on this occasion. He'd thought he'd heard it all, but he hadn't even been close.

However, it wasn't just the shock of hearing Rachel tell him that Karen was pregnant with his baby that stunned him. It wasn't true. It was the ramifications of Rachel's actions that left him feeling weak and sick to his stomach. Rachel hadn't seduced him, he realised, because she'd wanted to sleep with him. She hadn't even been desperate for a man. And to be honest, she hadn't actually slept with him. As soon as he'd performed to her satisfaction she'd found somewhere else to spend the night.

'Why are you looking at me like that?'

The revulsion he was feeling must have shown in his face. The sense of disgust, of betrayal at being used and discarded, must have communicated itself to her—because she'd left what she was doing and was now facing him again.

Jack's lips curled. 'Do you need to ask?'

'What?' She was defensive. 'You didn't think Karen would tell me she was expecting a baby? Oh, yes, she was very proud of it. How could you, Jack? How could you let her come here and ask me to give you a divorce?'

'That's crap and you know it,' he snapped. 'If Karen's pregnant, it's nothing to do with me. But don't think I don't know what you're trying to do now. You're trying to divert me from what you did last night. You didn't seduce me because you wanted me,' he persisted when she would have interrupted him. 'You didn't even seduce me because you wanted sex. You believed that woman's lies and you decided to teach me a lesson. And if, in the process, you got pregnant, you were prepared to risk that just to gain the upper hand.'

CHAPTER FIVE

THE BROWN ENVELOPE, with the words 'Private and Confidential' printed on it in bold letters, was lying on Jack's desk when he arrived at the office.

He guessed Harry, who always sorted the post, had put it there because of its personal connotations. In the normal way, all the mail was delivered to his personal assistant. Myrna opened the letters, dealt with those she could, and put the rest aside for his attention.

Jack studied the envelope for a few moments before picking it up. He'd guessed what it was, and he couldn't prevent the sudden acceleration of his pulse. It was all very well assuring himself that the heart specialist he'd seen almost three weeks ago had been of the opinion that overwork, stress, and his unhealthy lifestyle were the most likely cause of the symptoms Jack was suffering. Assurances didn't help him to sleep at night, or convince him that the tests the specialist had arranged were simply to ease his mind.

It was over a week since he'd been admitted to the private clinic in Plymouth and subjected to an intensive examination of his heart. An exercise cardiogram hadn't satisfied the cardiologist, and so an intravenous line had been inserted into one of the blood vessels in his groin and a kind of dye had been injected that showed up on an X-ray machine.

It had all been slightly unreal and slightly embarrassing, and he'd wished like hell there'd been someone that he could confide his anxieties to. But since the row he and Rachel had had the afternoon after they'd had sex they weren't even speaking to one another. He knew she was unlikely to apologise; she didn't think she'd done anything wrong. And he didn't see why he should have to beg her to believe Karen Johnson meant nothing to him. Dammit, what kind of a lech did she think he was?

They were at an impasse, and one that wasn't helped by his current preoccupation with his health. He hated the feeling of not being in command of his body, resented like mad the knowledge that he'd given doctors and specialists the right to take control of his life. He might even have found it in his heart to forgive Rachel if he hadn't felt so bloody scared.

Deciding there was no point in delaying the inevitable any longer, he picked up the envelope and used the silver letter opener Rachel had given him to slit the flap. Then, with the tips of his fingers, he pulled out the official report.

It *was* from a private clinic. The name of the clinic was printed neatly across the top. 'Cairns Gynaecological Consultancy' it announced, just above the heading that read, *'Result of Examination (Pregnancy)'*.

'What the—'

Jack swore, staring at the sheet in front of him with disbelieving eyes. The report stated that an examination had been carried out three days ago on Ms Karen Johnson. The result was positive. According to the gynaecologist who'd signed the report, Ms Johnson was approximately sixteen weeks into term.

Sixteen weeks!

Jack flung the report down upon his desk as if it had burned him. Then he snatched it up again, scanning the heading for an address or telephone number. Both were there, indicating that the clinic which had performed the test was in Torquay. Evidently Karen had had her condition authenticated to prove she was telling the truth.

But it wasn't *his* child!

Jack blew out a shaky breath, feeling the familiar threads of dizziness weaving in and out of his consciousness as he struggled to make sense of what Karen was trying to do. Destroy his marriage, certainly. That went without saying. But surely she knew she couldn't get away with this?

They had *not* had an affair. He hadn't even slept with her. The only reason he hadn't reported her harassment to the authorities before was because he'd felt some gratitude towards her. The night he'd taken her out to dinner had been the night he'd had his first serious attack of dizziness. But had the fact that he'd passed out on her doorstep anything to do with this?

He'd been experiencing odd symptoms for some time—bouts of breathlessness and an accelerating heartbeat that he'd put down to the hectic pace of his work. Since he and Rachel had stopped sleeping together—stopped doing anything together, he conceded grimly—he'd begun spending more and more time at the office. He exercised little, probably ate all the wrong food, and generally lived a life that was governed by stress.

But passing out on Karen's doorstep had been his wake-up call. He'd come round to find himself lying on her sofa, his jacket discarded, his tie loosened, and feeling like the biggest fool in the world.

Of course he'd pretended it was because he'd had too much to drink, but Karen must have known he'd barely touched the wine he'd ordered to have with dinner. That was when fear had become his constant companion, and he'd have said anything to hide how he really felt.

Taking him at his word, Karen had insisted he spend the night on the sofa. He wasn't fit to drive, she'd said, and short of telling her the truth Jack had had no argument to offer. It was only now that he wondered if her proposal had been less than innocent. Had she already had this scenario in mind? Had she guessed he was unlikely to ask her out again?

His mouth felt unpleasantly dry, and he got up and went into the adjoining bathroom to fill a glass with water from the tap. Staring at his reflection in the mirror above the hand basin, he wasn't surprised to see he looked haggard. He felt haggard, dammit. But when he'd slammed down the phone on Karen's outrageous claim two weeks ago he'd never expected she'd try anything like this.

She wasn't pregnant. Since she'd taken the test two days ago Rachel had hardly been able to think of anything else, but whatever way she looked at the cartridge, the desired coloured dot didn't pop up in the window.

She'd been convinced she was pregnant. After the night she and Jack had spent together she'd been sure the claim she'd made to Karen Johnson would no longer be a lie. It had always happened before. That was one of the reasons why she'd turned Jack away when he'd attempted to resume a normal relationship after her last miscarriage. That and the fact that she'd felt so devastated, so inadequate as a woman. And totally incapable of doing anything that might risk her getting pregnant again.

But now she had risked it, and it hadn't worked. Well, not after one night, anyway. And she couldn't be absolutely sure she'd got pregnant the first time she and Jack had made love. In the early stages of their relationship, as Jack had said, they hadn't been able to keep their hands off one another.

She shivered. What now? She'd been thinking about nothing else, but was she really going to risk Jack's rejecting her just to prove a point? Jack had already guessed what she'd attempted and he despised her for it.

So what was she going to do? She was finding it incredibly difficult to concentrate on anything, and the fact that Jack hadn't broached the subject again surely proved that what she'd suspected all along was true. He was involved with the other woman.

Right now she was in her studio, where she usually spent her time, trying to devise the artwork for her latest commission, *Benjie's Big Day*. She'd been the illustrator for the Benjie books for two years, ever since the author had started writing them, and until now she'd always found an escape from her problems in her work. But not today.

A sound alerted her to the fact that she was no longer alone, and, turning, she expected to find Mrs Grady behind her, offering tea or a cool drink. But it wasn't Mrs Grady. Her husband was leaning against the arched frame of the door, a look of undisguised weariness on his face.

'Oh, it's you,' she said, her surprise at seeing him there making her forget they weren't talking to one another. Then, because he looked so hollow-eyed and drawn, she added warily, 'Are you all right?'

Jack made a disparaging sound. 'Is that your way of telling me I look rough?'

'No.' Rachel defended herself automatically. 'You do look—tired.' She waited a beat. 'Obviously you're not getting enough sleep.'

'Like you care,' he said tightly.

Rachel stiffened. 'If you choose to spend your nights screwing your mistress, why should I be expected to care?'

'I don't spend my nights screwing anyone,' he corrected her, enunciating his words carefully so there could be no mistake, but Rachel only gave him a scornful look.

'Then how else is Karen pregnant?' she demanded, and he sighed.

'I've told you, that has nothing to do with me—'

'You *would* say that,' she countered. 'What's the matter? Conscience troubling you?'

Jack was too exhausted to argue. 'Look,' he said, 'as a matter of fact I've not been feeling so good. That's why I'm home at—' he glanced at his watch '—at four o'clock in the afternoon.'

Rachel felt an instinctive twinge of anxiety. She couldn't help it. But she determinedly squashed it and turned back to her painting. 'Ask Mrs Grady if she has any aspirin,' she said, striving for indifference. 'As I say, you'll probably feel better if you get to bed at a reasonable hour for once.'

Jack had to acknowledge that was a fair point. Lately he'd reverted to spending more and more time at his desk, despite the warnings he'd been given. But, hell, he wasn't welcome at home, and the company apartment was bloody lonely. In his present condition he'd rather have the company of the office cleaner than spend the whole evening on his own.

Considering his words before speaking, he said, 'I don't think aspirin's going to do it somehow.' He gave a wry grimace and turned away. 'But thanks for your concern, Rachel. It means a lot.'

The door to the studio had been open when he arrived, and he left it open now, starting back across the lawn towards the house. To hell with her, he thought, anger overtaking propitiation. He didn't know why he'd ever imagined she'd be interested in how he was feeling. She'd made it clear what she really thought of him the morning after she'd practically screwed his brains out.

'Wait!'

He had reached the patio doors when he heard her calling him. Obviously her conscience was pricking her, he thought bitterly. Or maybe she was just the tiniest bit ashamed of the way she'd behaved. Either way, she was coming after him, and despite his resentment he paused to allow her to catch up.

Almost objectively—and certainly against his better judgment—he allowed himself to study her appearance. Unlike him, she looked good, the blush of a golden tan giving colour to her bare arms and legs. She was wearing a pink cropped top, whose narrow straps gave him a glimpse of a dusky cleavage, and a short white pleated miniskirt that exposed her long slim legs.

Jack wondered if it was only the memory of the night they'd spent together that made him so aware of everything about her. Had he really forgotten how sexy she was, how passionate she could be? Or was it the fear that he might be losing her that filled him with such a sense of panic? If his heart condition didn't finish him off, the result of Karen Johnson's antics just might.

Not saying anything, he arched an enquiring brow in Rachel's direction. If she had something to say, he decided it might be wiser to wait and see what it was. And, dammit, she had taken advantage of him, whatever justification she thought she'd had. All the same, he didn't want to talk about it now.

'What did you mean?' Rachel asked, looping her hair back behind her ears and looking into his face with troubled eyes. 'When you said you didn't think an aspirin would do it?'

'Did I say that?' Jack could feel the heat bearing down on his shoulders, his jacket like a dead weight on his sweating frame. 'Don't give it another thought,' he said, stepping gratefully into the coolness of the drawing room. He ran a slightly unsteady hand over his damp forehead. 'I think I need a shower.'

Rachel tugged her lower lip between her teeth, not satisfied with the glibness of his answer. 'You said you weren't feeling well,' she persisted. 'Is something wrong?'

'What could be wrong?' Jack was glad that he was out of the blazing sun as his senses swam. God, he so much didn't want to make a fool of himself in front of her. 'I guess I'm just feeling under the weather, that's all.'

Yeah, right.

'There's nothing wrong at the office, is there?' Rachel wasn't satisfied. She followed him into the drawing room, averting her eyes from the sofa where Karen had sat and looking at Jack instead. 'I know getting that contract with Carlyle's wasn't easy, and if it's something to do with the company I'd be glad to help if I can.'

'You're all heart.'

Jack was sardonic, but he couldn't help it. Yeah, he was having problems, but they were not of a professional nature. Since he'd read the gynaecologist's report that he'd found on his desk that morning he hadn't been able to think of anything else. And as for telling Rachel about it? Dear God, he'd rather stick pins in his eyes.

'Look, it's nothing,' he said now, not wanting to get into a discussion. He felt shattered, but even if he took her advice and rested for a while he doubted he'd be able to relax. Dammit, he had a mad woman stalking his every move, insisting she was having his baby. The DNA test that would prove she was lying would be done eventually, but until then she could easily go on wreaking havoc in his life. 'I'll see you later on.'

'And *do* you have any aspirin?'

Aspirin!

Jack stifled a groan. 'Yeah, I've got aspirin,' he answered, heading across the room towards the hall doorway. 'Anyway, I'll probably feel better after I've had a shower.'

Rachel moistened her dry lips. 'Um—I won't be around later,' she murmured, and Jack paused to glance back at her.

'No?'

'No.' Rachel twisted the hem of her silk top between nervous fingers, inadvertently exposing the dusky hollow of her navel. 'I've arranged to go out.'

'Oh.'

Jack nodded, acknowledging he'd heard her, but his eyes were drawn to the soft curve of her stomach. Her shorts were low on her hips and he could see the gentle indentation of her waist. And although his head was swimming, he felt his body stir.

Fighting for control, he was forced to accept that since the night they'd slept together he'd found it hard to ignore her. Despite his finer feelings—anger, resentment, bitterness— he couldn't stop thinking of how she'd felt beneath him, how soft her skin had been, how tightly she'd curled around him.

He realised that the months of their estrangement must have created a dam on his emotions. He'd been forced to stop thinking of her in that way, and slowly but surely his body had been schooled to meet the circumstances. Now that dam had been breached and he was vulnerable. All the feelings he'd suppressed were suddenly swamping him with their needs.

But it wasn't going to happen. With a muffled, 'Right,' he practically stumbled out of the door. He needed to get away, to find somewhere to lick his wounds in private. If he could just get upstairs to his room without falling flat on his face.

'I've arranged to have dinner with Lucy.'

As Jack was starting up the stairs, clinging desperately to the banister, Rachel came out of the drawing room and stood watching him. She must have decided he deserved an explanation, and she was obviously waiting for some response from him.

'Lucy. Right,' he said again, wishing she would just go back to her studio. 'Don't forget to give her my love.'

That achieved the purpose it had been intended for. With a muffled exclamation, Rachel turned and disappeared from view. She and Lucy Robards had spent a lot of time together in recent months, and she knew that Jack and her friend cordially despised one another. A divorcee herself, Lucy had never shown anything but contempt for him.

Outside again, Rachel was surprised to find she was feeling bruised and tearful. Dammit, she thought, she didn't owe him any explanations, so why had she bothered to tell him where she was going and who she was going to be with? Why couldn't she have let him stew in his own juice, let him wonder if she'd started dating again? It would serve him right after what he was putting her through.

The truth was, she'd felt sorry for him. Yes, she knew she was stupid, but that didn't alter the way he made her feel. If he was ill, she wanted to know about it. She was still his wife, however easily he was able to forget *his* vows.

And what had he meant by looking at her in that way? She hadn't been ignorant of the fact that his eyes had dropped so significantly below her waist. For a man who was reputedly feeling 'under the weather', he'd shown far too much interest in her body. Nor could she ignore the flood of heat and wetness she could still feel between her legs.

She stomped into her studio, feeling hot and antsy. He must have done that deliberately, she thought. He must have guessed how she'd feel when he'd let those disturbing green eyes assess her with so little respect. But it was her fault for letting him think she wanted him. He was punishing her for sleeping with her husband. And how ironic was that?

She had to remember Karen, remember she was expecting his baby. Instead of playing with the idea of repeating the offence, she should be considering what she was going to do. But, dear God, how could she even *think* of divorcing him when she still loved him? If only she'd been pregnant, she thought. Then their marriage might have stood a chance...

CHAPTER SIX

RACHEL MADE SURE she left the house before Jack came downstairs again.

As soon as she was sure he'd be in the shower, she locked up her studio and went back to the house to speak to Mrs Grady. She wanted to be certain the housekeeper knew that Jack would be in for supper. Leaving him to explain the position would have given him far too much of an advantage.

Upstairs in her room, Rachel stripped off her clothes and stepped into the shower herself. The cool water felt good on her hot skin, and she felt infinitely fresher when she came out. Riffling through her wardrobe, she pulled out a chiffon-sleeved dress of dark green silk jersey. Its wraparound style accentuated her curves and left a satisfying length of bare leg exposed.

Her newly washed hair swung thickly to her shoulders, and, shunning a necklace, she threaded wide gold hoops through her ears. A matching jumble of thin gold bracelets clinked on her wrist, balancing her watch, and ankle-breaking heels completed her ensemble.

She studied her reflection in the long cheval mirror when she was ready, wondering why she'd gone to so much trouble. She was only having dinner with Lucy, for heaven's sake. She'd even told Jack what she was doing— a situation she would have revised now, if she could.

It was just a ten-minute walk to Lucy's house, but Rachel took her car. Although it was summer, and at present there were plenty of people about, it would probably be dark when she came home, and the cliff path could be rather scary at night.

Her friend lived in the second of a row of semi-detached homes on the outskirts of Market Abbas. Rachel's father's company had built the houses in the days before Jack had come to work for him. At that time Fox Construction had been a comparatively small operation, tendering for house extensions and occasionally a small estate. It wasn't until Jack had suggested expanding into the commercial market that the company had really taken off.

But she didn't want to think of Jack's contribution to the financial security her father had enjoyed in the latter days of his life. Better to remember what Karen had said about him only marrying her to get control of the company. She didn't really believe it. With his talent for business, Jack would have succeeded anywhere. But was that what other people had thought when he married her? The sting of that suspicion would take a long time to go away.

Lucy was working at her computer when Rachel rang her doorbell. 'Come in,' she called. 'I won't be a minute.' And Rachel stepped gratefully into the hall of the small house. 'I'm just answering emails,' Lucy added, using the mouse to send the last reply she'd written on its way. As well as writing a food column for a Plymouth newspaper, Lucy was also the agony aunt on several national magazines—a fact that Jack had always said, with some humour, he found very hard to believe.

'Hey, you look stunning!' Lucy exclaimed now, swinging round in her chair and regarding her friend with assessing eyes. 'Did I forget something? I thought we were just going to have a pizza in town.'

'We are.' Rachel felt her colour deepen with embarrassment. 'I—I just felt like dressing up, that's all. Do you mind?'

'Well, it makes my jeans and shirt look a little dowdy,' remarked Lucy, glancing ruefully down at her outfit. 'If I'd known we were dressing up I'd have worn something different than this.'

'You look fine,' said Rachel earnestly, wishing she hadn't made such an effort with her appearance. But after that conversation with Jack she'd wanted to do something to give her back her confidence in herself.

'If you say so.'

Lucy shrugged and got to her feet, revealing she was several inches shorter than her friend. Rachel's shoes didn't help, but it was too late to worry about that now. And Lucy *did* look attractive. Her tight-fitting jeans and fringed suede shirt were a perfect foil for her straight black bob and strongly feminine features.

'You drove,' she said, glancing out of the window of her office and seeing Rachel's sleek Audi parked at the kerb. Then she grimaced. 'Of course. You could hardly walk here in those heels.'

'I can walk,' said Rachel defensively, not really liking Lucy in this mood. It was as if Lucy was annoyed with her because she'd worn something flattering for a change. Usually, because Lucy was a success in so many ways, Rachel was the one who felt inferior.

'Anyway, it will save me getting my car out of the garage,' Lucy went on, as if Rachel hadn't spoken. 'I'll just get my bag.'

It was a twenty-minute drive into Plymouth, made longer by the traffic heading into the city for the evening. Lucy said little on the journey, allowing Rachel to concentrate on her driving, and it wasn't until they were parked near the famous Hoe that she said, 'Where's Jack tonight?'

'Jack?' Rachel repeated his name to give herself time to consider her answer. 'He—er—he's at home, actually. He came home early. He wasn't feeling well, or so he said.'

Lucy blew out a breath. 'I assume you've had no more word from this woman he's been running around with?' She frowned. 'Karen something or other, didn't you say?'

'Johnson,' said Rachel, half wishing she'd never mentioned the woman's appearance to Lucy. But in the aftermath of Karen's visit she'd had to talk to someone. Thankfully, she hadn't told her friend everything—like the fact that Karen had said she was pregnant. Or that she, Rachel, had seduced her husband that same night, a circumstance Lucy would find hard to condone after she'd sworn she'd never let him near her again.

'Yeah, Johnson,' Lucy said now, linking arms with Rachel as they walked up the street to the restaurant. She glanced sideways at her. 'You haven't seen her again, have you?' she persisted. 'You seem awfully reticent on the subject.'

'Of course I haven't seen her again.' Rachel managed to inject a note of conviction into her voice. 'Why would I? She's said what she came to say.'

'Which was?'

'You know.' Rachel was dismissive. 'That I should give Jack a divorce so that he can marry her.'

'And what does Jack have to say about it?' Lucy waited for her response, and when it wasn't immediately forthcoming she went on, 'You *have* spoken to him about it? You haven't conveniently forgotten about it, like you tend to do with things you don't like?'

Rachel gasped. 'Like what?'

'Well, like the fact that you found out about this affair six months ago but it wasn't until this Johnson woman turned up at the house that you began to take it seriously.'

'That's not true!' Rachel was indignant.

'So why are you still together?'

That stumped her. 'Well—because I wasn't sure it was true.'

'Not true?' They had reached the restaurant, and Lucy waited until they were seated at a table in the corner before continuing, 'He spends the night at her house, you've even seen the CCTV pictures of them entering the company apartment together, and you say you're not certain. What do you need, Rachel? You just don't want to face the consequences, that's all.'

Thankfully, the appearance of their waiter for the evening prevented any further accusations from Lucy. In discussing what to drink, and the specials available but not listed on the menu, Rachel was able to avoid an immediate response. She just wished Lucy would take the hint and get off the subject. No matter how good a friend she was, she didn't have the right to browbeat her like this.

They each chose lasagne, with a chilled jug of the house wine to accompany the meal. Rachel couldn't help but notice that the waiter was especially attentive to her this evening, and it went some way to restoring the confidence Lucy's scornful comments had destroyed.

'I just don't understand you,' Lucy confessed, as they ate a green salad to start their meal. 'Here you are: you're bright, you're beautiful—'

'Gee, thanks.'

'—and you're financially independent,' Lucy continued doggedly. 'And that's without taking your share of the business into account. You don't need Jack Riordan, Rachel. In my opinion, you never should have married him in the first place.'

Rachel cast her a resigned look. 'So what do I do? Divorce him?'

'That would be the most sensible thing, yeah.' Lucy smiled, but it wasn't a pleasant sight. 'And I'd take him to the cleaners for every rotten penny he's got.'

'Force him to leave the company, you mean?'

'If that's what it takes.'

Rachel shook her head. 'I couldn't do that.'

'Why not?'

'Well, because the shareholders would never agree to it, for one thing. And for another, Jack *is* Fox Construction. Without his flair, his insight, the company would have been bought out long ago. My father wasn't a businessman, Lucy. He was a tradesman. He enjoyed what he was doing, but it wasn't until Jack came to him with his ideas that he saw how successful they could be.'

'You don't think it might have been easier for Jack because it wasn't *his* money he was spending?' Lucy ventured carelessly, and Rachel stiffened.

'What are you saying? That he only married me to get his hands on Fox Construction?' She'd heard that before—from Karen—and it pained her that Lucy should think the same.

However, her friend seemed to realise she'd gone too far, and she quickly backtracked. 'Of course not,' she protested, reaching across the table to squeeze Rachel's hand. 'Jack loved you. You know that. But, like all successful men, he got greedy. A wife's not enough for him. He wants a mistress on the side.'

Rachel sighed. 'As Martin did?'

Lucy's lips tightened. 'Since you mention it,' she said, 'exactly as Martin did.' She scowled. 'And I was fool enough to believe him when he said he wanted an amicable divorce.' She shook her head. 'The bastard emptied our bank accounts, Rachel, and then pleaded poverty to the authorities. God, if I'd known Debbie was pregnant I'd never have let him get away with it.'

Rachel felt a shiver of apprehension slide down her spine at her friend's words. She'd forgotten all the details of Lucy's separation—the lies Martin had told to get a judge to give him the right to live in the house he'd previously shared with his wife. That was why Lucy had been reduced to living in a small rented semi in Market Abbas instead of in the comfortable five-bedroom home she and Martin had bought when they got married.

'You don't believe me, do you?'

Lucy was persistent, and Rachel's head was beginning to ache with the constant barrage of advice. 'Look,' she said, 'this is my problem, right? I've got to deal with it. It's good of you to be concerned about me, but I need to handle this in my own way.'

'Suit yourself.'

At last Lucy seemed to get the message, and for the rest of the evening Rachel steered clear of anything that might remind her of their earlier conversation. Once again she was grateful that she hadn't told Lucy Karen was expecting a baby. The comparison with the break-up of her own marriage would have been just too obvious to ignore.

* * *

Jack spent the evening switching channels on the wide-screen TV in the den. The room had originally started out as a family room, but without the expected influx of young children it had acquired bookshelves and a writing bureau, as well as an entertainment console.

Rachel often used the room as a second studio. It was large and high-ceilinged, and it had good light. In colder weather, particularly if there was snow on the ground, it was easier for her to work indoors.

Tonight, however, the room seemed unusually quiet. Even with the television playing it felt abandoned and remote from human contact. Much like himself, he thought, hesitating only a moment before reaching for the bottle of single malt he'd brought in with him. Who really cared if he killed himself? he reflected. Rachel might be better off without him.

It was only a little after half-past-nine when he heard the Audi's engine. It had a distinctive sound, different from the Ford Mrs Grady sometimes drove. He couldn't believe it. When Rachel had dinner with Lucy Robards she was rarely back before eleven or eleven-thirty. He knew because he'd lain awake many a night waiting for her to come home.

He wanted to stay where he was and ignore her. To pretend he was so interested in the documentary that was being screened at this moment that he hadn't heard her come in. But the fear that she might go upstairs without seeing him was paramount. Ignoring the tell-tale flutter of his heart, he opened the door.

Rachel was standing in the hall, putting her keys away in her purse, when she caught sight of him. The expression that crossed her face at that moment was hardly flattering, but Jack refused to be put off. She looked marvellous, the slinky dress she was wearing accentuating every sensuous curve of her slender body. It crossed his mind that she was dressed too sexily to have been having dinner with only Lucy. Had that woman organised a cosy foursome with some of her newspaper colleagues? Surely not, he thought bitterly. He suspected Lucy Robards would chew nails before allowing another man into her life.

All the same, seeing Rachel like this reminded him of the way she'd looked when he'd come home and found her practically naked. When he'd thought the house was on fire—only to get burned up himself. God, she'd been so beautiful, so desirable; it gave him a hard-on just to think of it. Or was his body reacting to present forces, the knowledge that she was his wife and, God help him! he still wanted her?

'Did you want something?' Rachel asked now, tucking her purse under her arm, making him envy the small pouch pressed hard against her soft breast.

'You're early,' Jack said lamely, wondering what she'd do if he invited her to have a drink with him in the den. Probably say that she was tired, he decided. She certainly didn't look very friendly.

'Lucy was tired,' Rachel said, not altogether truthfully. In actual fact it was she who had used that excuse, not her friend. Then, because she couldn't ignore how he looked, so pale and hollow-eyed, she asked, 'How are you?' She despised herself for feeling sorry for him, but she couldn't help it. 'Did Mrs Grady make you some supper?'

'Well, I didn't go out, if that's what you're asking,' said Jack, trying to calm his rampant libido. For God's sake, in his state his sexual urges should be easy to control. But they weren't. Then, recklessly, he said, 'Come and have a drink. I'd welcome the company. I've not spoken to a soul except Mrs Grady all evening.'

'Not even Karen?' Rachel couldn't prevent the provocative rejoinder, and she saw the look of frustration that crossed his dark face.

'Not anyone,' he repeated, realising how impossible it would be to tell her about the report Karen had sent him now. It probably wasn't such a good idea to spend time alone with Rachel either. In his present weakened condition it would be far too easy to make mistakes.

He was about to say, *Forget it,* when she beat him to it. 'All right,' she said, lifting her slim shoulders in a careless gesture of dismissal. 'I'll have a drink with you.' She walked towards him, taking off first one shoe and then the other. Then, lifting them to eye level by their straps, she added, 'You don't mind, do you?'

Jack gave a careful shake of his head, relieved when the action didn't cause his senses to swim. Backing up against the door, he allowed her to pass him, her perfume surrounding him as she did so, warm and fragrant, overlaid with the fresh, womanly scent of her body.

As he followed her into the room and turned off the television he wondered why she'd suddenly decided to humour him. A month ago she wouldn't have hesitated before making some puerile excuse and heading up to her bedroom. But then, a month ago he'd have had more sense than to offer the invitation.

It was dark outside, and before doing anything else Jack switched on the pair of floor lights that stood at either end of the bookshelves. There was already a lamp burning on the bureau, and the room looked suddenly more attractive in the mellow light.

'Sorry—no candles,' he said shortly, knowing it was a loaded comment, but she didn't take offence.

'You liked them?' she asked, immediately putting him

on the defensive again, and Jack had to take a steadying breath before replying.

He didn't honestly know if the fact that his heart was doing flip-flops was her fault or his, but he had to calm down. 'They were—different,' he said, hoping that wouldn't elicit another disturbing reminiscence of that night. He crossed the room and determinedly picked up the bottle of single malt. 'I've got Scotch, or Scotch and water. Or I can get you something else from the fridge. Wine, perhaps? Your choice.'

'Scotch is fine,' said Rachel, perching on the edge of the armchair where he'd been sitting earlier and massaging her aching soles. 'Mmm, that's much better.'

Trying to ignore the fact that when she rested her foot across her knee her legs parted and her skirt rode enticingly high on her thighs, Jack found a second glass and splashed an inch of Scotch into it. 'Water?'

'I'll take it straight,' she said, looking up at him through her lashes. Her fingers brushed his as she took the glass. 'Thanks.'

Jack turned away, recklessly refilling his own glass. But even the smell caused a distinct shortness of breath, and he put it down again. Then, because it would have been too unsettling to sit opposite her, he made do with hooking his hip onto a corner of the bureau.

Needing to normalise the situation, he said, 'Did you have a pleasant evening?'

'It was okay.' In all honesty Rachel couldn't say she'd enjoyed it.

'It was just you and Lucy, right?'

Rachel frowned. What was that supposed to mean? 'Yes,' she replied warily. 'I told you what I was doing before I went out.'

'Mmm.' Jack crossed his arms, his tee shirt tightening across his broad shoulders. 'I just wondered.'

'Wondered what?'

Jack knew he shouldn't have said anything. He really didn't want to get into an argument with her. Take it easy, he told himself. Think what you're saying before you open your big mouth. 'Nothing,' he muttered now, reaching behind him for his glass and then remembering he shouldn't have any more. 'Is your drink all right?'

'It's whisky,' Rachel said drily. 'I don't think even *you* could louse it up.' She paused, considering. 'Why did you ask if Lucy and I were on our own?'

Jack stifled a groan. 'No reason.'

'Oh, come on.' Rachel wasn't buying that. 'Nobody asks a question for no reason.' She hesitated. 'Did you think I had a date?'

'No.' Jack tried for indignation, but when that didn't work he said wearily, 'All right. Maybe I did. You have to admit you don't usually make such an effort when you're going out with her.'

Rachel's eyes widened. 'You noticed?' she said mockingly. She stretched out her slim legs, making no effort to push her skirt down. 'Do you think I look nice?'

Nice wasn't even adequate, but Jack wasn't going to tell her that. It obviously amused her to provoke him, and if he had any sense he'd ignore it. The trouble was, there seemed to be some kind of blockage between his brain and his sex.

'Yeah, you look nice,' he said tightly, a reluctant smile hovering about his mouth. 'Very glamorous. Very sexy.'

Rachel's lips parted, but whether it was because she was surprised at the compliment or simply continuing the game she seemed to be playing, Jack couldn't be sure. Whatever, when her tongue appeared to wet her lower lip he felt the jolt of his reaction spread like wildfire through his body.

'You look nice, too,' she said, convincing him she was only toying with him. 'You always looked good in jeans.'

Yeah. Jack swallowed. The trouble was, they were bloody tight, bloody revealing at the moment, and he was glad that the angle of the bureau prevented her from seeing what she was doing to him. 'Thanks,' he said, not meaning it. 'So—where did you have dinner?'

It was another attempt to turn the conversation into safer channels, but Rachel seemed determined not to oblige him. 'Oh, we had lasagne at Romano's,' she declared offhandedly. 'How about you? You look a little flushed. Are you sure you're not coming down with something?'

Jack couldn't prevent a snort of frustration now. 'What's with all the concern?' he asked. 'A few hours ago you were telling me I shouldn't expect you to care how I was feeling. Now suddenly you're Florence Nightingale! I'd like to know what's caused this sudden change of heart. Do you feel guilty, or what?'

'Why should I feel guilty?' Despite her determination not to let him get to her, his words caught her on the raw. 'I can't help being concerned about you. You're my husband.'

Now it was Jack's turn to look surprised. 'Yeah, right,' he said sceptically. 'And when did you remember that, exactly?'

'I've never forgotten it,' retorted Rachel, faint colour rising up her throat. 'I'm not the one who's been playing away.'

'Nor am I,' said Jack harshly, relieved to be back on more familiar ground, but Rachel had other ideas.

'In any case, I thought I proved how I felt a couple of weeks ago.'

'It's almost three weeks since we—connected,' he said, using that word deliberately. 'And I don't think remembering I was your husband had anything to do with that. You wanted to prove you could make me want you—and what do you know? You succeeded. But don't get too excited, baby. It would have taken a stronger man than me to refuse that invitation.'

Rachel's face burned now. 'You can't help being objectionable, can you?' she snapped. Slamming her glass down onto an end table, she got abruptly to her feet. 'I don't know why I agreed to have a drink with you. I felt sorry for you, I suppose. But that was stupid, because you don't need anyone's sympathy. You're completely heartless!'

I wish.

Jack knew a moment's regret, but he refused to let her have the final word. Moving into her path, he said softly, 'I'm sorry. That was mean.' He looked over her shoulder. 'Don't go. You haven't even finished your drink.'

'You finish it,' muttered Rachel resentfully, but she didn't push past him, and before he could think what he was doing, Jack slipped his arms about her waist.

It was a mistake. He knew that as soon as he felt the silky fabric of her dress beneath his hands. Smooth and slippery, it moved against her skin, revealing she was wearing little underneath. And, although only moments before she'd been angry with him, she did nothing to stop his hands from sliding down over her hips to the provocative curve of her bottom.

The dress was absurdly short, and he was tempted to find the hem and explore beneath it. Bare golden skin invited him to do it, and when he let one hand entwine in her hair she tilted her face up without resistance.

It would be so easy, he thought, and his groin ached in

anticipation. So easy to lift the hem and forget everything in that hot wet place between her legs. He wanted to. God, his erection was fighting his jeans for supremacy, and in spite of what she'd said before he touched her he had the feeling Rachel wouldn't object.

But that was her intention, he realised. The eyes she'd turned up to his were no longer resentful, but eager and expectant, as if she knew exactly what he was thinking. And he knew in that moment why she'd agreed to have a drink with him. However unlikely it seemed, she wanted him to make love to her again.

But why? Why? As his pulse ebbed and flowed with the effort of trying to control his emotions, he wondered if the little scheme she'd engineered hadn't worked and she'd decided to try again.

It was crazy, but it was obvious she thought he was putty in her hands. Even the dress she'd worn was designed to slip easily off her shoulders, and if she was wearing any underwear it would be as skimpy and erotic as he remembered from before.

His heart skipped one beat, then another. Trying for distraction, he told himself he could do this—or rather pretend to. Why shouldn't he humour her? It wouldn't be the first time he'd withdrawn and spent himself elsewhere.

'Are you going to kiss me?'

Rachel was gazing up at him, but her face seemed to be wavering in front of his eyes. 'Why not?' he muttered, not sure whether he was answering her question or his, and lowering his head he allowed his lips to brush against her soft mouth.

She was all fire and heat, her tongue darting to meet his with an urgency that spoke of her own desires, her own needs. Her hands were all over him, reaching for his face, nails curling into the damp hair at his nape, slipping down between them to pull his tee shirt up and find the bare skin of his stomach.

He couldn't help himself. He leaned into her, deepening the kiss, indulging himself in the sensual hunger she was creating. Her bare leg brushed against his calf, performed a crazy little caress before wrapping itself around him. She leaned in closer and he felt her rubbing herself against his throbbing sex.

God! A wave of sweat enveloped him, and as she fumbled with the button at his waist he felt his senses swim dangerously close to the edge. He couldn't breathe; for a moment he was sure his heart had stopped beating altogether, and the need for survival overcame all else.

Tearing her hands from his zip, he managed to stagger back from her. He didn't know how he looked. Pretty ghastly, he suspected, but Rachel wasn't looking for reasons.

'You bastard!' she swore, evidently unaware of what was happening to him. 'I should have expected something like this. You have to win, don't you, Jack? One way or the other.'

Jack fought for breath. 'You don't understand—' he choked, but she wasn't interested in explanations.

'Oh, yes, I do,' she retorted, not prepared to listen to anything he had to say. 'Get out of my way, damn you!' she snapped, pushing him aside without hesitation, marching out of the room with as much pride as she could muster in bare feet.

CHAPTER SEVEN

DESPITE FEELING LESS than one hundred per cent, Jack left for the office early the next morning. He'd slept badly, but that wasn't new. These days his good nights were few and far between. He'd never considered what made people hypochondriacs until he'd been faced with his present predicament. But there was no doubt that his fluttering pulse and the dizziness made him supremely conscious of every breath he took when he was in bed.

He reached his office without encountering anyone but Harry. He'd collected a cup of coffee on the way, and sat down at his desk to drink it. It probably wasn't the most sensible thing to drink after last night's little fiasco. But, what the hell? He had to have some stimulation in his life.

He thanked God now that Rachel hadn't been aware of what was happening. She might have been angry with him—scrub that, she *was* angry with him—but he'd have been mortified if she'd known her pathetic push had driven him to his knees.

If he'd harboured any doubts that what the doctors had told him was true, last night had delivered a rude awakening. He'd been warned to slow down, to avoid stress and over-stimulation, but he'd just continued on his merry way, refusing to believe his problems wouldn't go away on their own. Now he believed it.

So what was he going to do? Delegate his work to someone else and take a prolonged rest? That was one of the recommendations he'd been given before they'd started all these tests and examinations. In the days when he'd been certain he could handle this on his own.

A knock at the door caused him to stiffen. But it was only Harry who, as well as sorting the post, worked as doorman as well. 'Another letter for you, Mr Riordan,' he said, handing over an ordinary business-sized envelope. 'You're an early bird this morning.'

'Yeah.' Jack managed a smile and took the white envelope reluctantly. What now? he wondered, feeling his heart beating heavily in his chest.

'Seems like you could do with a lie-in now and again,' Harry commented, with the familiarity of long service. 'You're looking tired, Mr Riordan. You need a holiday. All these high-pressure deals are wearing you out.'

Jack took a breath. 'Mr Fox seemed to manage okay. He was a lot older than me when he retired.'

Harry grimaced. 'Mr Fox never ran a business as big as this, Mr Riordan. When he started up it was just a small operation. I knew Bob Fox for over twenty years, and he never took on anything he couldn't handle.'

Jack pulled a face. 'What are you saying? That I can't handle it?'

'Hell, no, Mr Riordan. Pardon my language. Everyone knows that it wasn't until you came on the scene that the company really took off.' Harry's face was flushed now, but he wasn't finished. 'All I'm saying is, don't be overdoing it—if you know what I mean? I've seen younger men than you collapse under the strain of too much success.'

Jack's lips twisted into a wry smile. 'Thanks.'

'I mean it.' And Jack was sure he did. 'Now, I'll leave you to enjoy your coffee in peace. Just let me know if you want another. I've got my own pot in the basement, and although I say it myself it's as good as anything you'll buy from one of them fast food places.'

'I'm sure.'

Jack smiled a little more freely this time, and Harry gave him an old-fashioned salute before disappearing out the door.

When he'd gone, however, the letter had to be faced, and Jack didn't hesitate before ripping it open. He was firmly convinced it would be from Karen, and he got something of a shock when he realised it was from his own doctor.

He supposed he'd been expecting a report much like the one Karen's gynaecologist had sent him, and that was why he hadn't associated the letter with himself. Now, however, he saw it was from Dr Moore, inviting him to visit the surgery at two o'clock that afternoon to discuss the results of the examination he'd had.

He didn't know if that was good news or bad. Surely if it was bad news Dr Moore would have phoned him? Or perhaps not. Maybe the doctor thought a letter would put the whole situation on a more formal basis. And if he was going to deliver a cutting blow, wouldn't it be better to do it in his surgery, where he had all the necessary resuscitation equipment if it was required?

Whoa! At this point Jack put the letter aside and got up from his desk. Dammit, he *was* becoming a hypochondriac—already anticipating the worst when he had no real reason for doing so. God, if only he could phone Rachel and ask her what she thought, ask her to come with him.

But that was impossible, particularly after last night, and he accepted that for the foreseeable future he was on his own…

'You're going to do *what*?'

Rachel had been taken aback when Jack had arrived home from the office early two afternoons in a row, but that was nothing compared to the news he'd just imparted.

'I'm going to Ireland,' repeated Jack doggedly, standing in the doorway of her studio, much as he'd done the day before. Only this time there was a look of grim determination on his lean face. 'For a month. Six weeks, maybe. I need a break.'

Rachel was stunned. She put down her paintbrush and wiped her suddenly unsteady hands on a cloth. 'Are you going alone?'

Jack snorted. 'What do you mean by that? This isn't a holiday, Rachel.'

Rachel shook her head. 'So when did you decide this? I didn't even know you'd been in touch with your parents.'

He hadn't been—until this afternoon. But Rachel didn't need to know that.

'It was a snap decision,' he said, pushing a restless hand through his hair. 'I've been feeling a bit—below par, as you know. It will give me a chance to—to take stock.'

'But a *month!*' Rachel couldn't get past that reality. 'What about the business? Don't you have responsibilities, commitments?'

'Hey, thanks for your concern.' Jack was stung by the fact that her first thought had been for the company. 'It'll survive. It always has.'

Rachel looked discomforted. 'I didn't mean that the way it sounded,' she muttered. 'Of course I'm concerned about you.' She hesitated. 'I—I'd be concerned about anybody who felt they needed a month's time out from their normal routine. I just don't understand why you're doing this. Is it something to do with what happened be- tween—between us? Is this your way of telling me you want a divorce, after all?'

'No!' At least Jack could be honest about that. 'I—it's got nothing to do with our situation. But it will do us both good to have a breathing space. And Mum and Dad have invited us there dozens of times, but we've always cried off.'

'Invited *us*?'

'Me, then,' agreed Jack, acknowledging that the one time Rachel had accompanied him on a visit to Ireland it had not been a success. They'd already been occupying separate rooms, and Jude and Maggie Riordan had defi- nitely not approved of their son spending his nights sleep- ing in an armchair instead of sharing the old-fashioned four-poster with his wife. 'They miss seeing the family.'

'I suppose.'

Rachel accepted that that was true. Since Jack's parents had moved back to County Wexford, when his father had retired, they did miss their children and grandchildren. But the pretty whitewashed cottage they'd bought over- looking Lough Ryan always welcomed visitors, and Jack, being the eldest, was the favourite son.

'Anyway, George is going to take temporary control of the company,' Jack continued, as Rachel fretted over what his parents might say about her.

She was the only daughter-in-law who hadn't given them any grandchildren, and they probably didn't under- stand why she'd stopped sleeping with their son. What if he told them about Karen? What if he'd been lying and he *was* the father of Karen's baby? She could well imagine the Riordans being somewhat ambivalent about the outcome.

'Are you interested in any of this?'

Rachel realised suddenly that while she'd been staring blindly into space Jack had continued talking, and her cheeks deepened with embarrassed colour. 'Sorry,' she mumbled awkwardly. 'I was just thinking.' She ran her tongue over her dry lips, 'When are you planning on leaving?'

'At the end of the week.' Jack was terse. 'I can't go before then because I've promised to bring George up to speed. If he has any problems he can always reach me anyway. I'll have my laptop with me, and it's easy enough to keep in touch.'

Rachel lifted her shoulders. 'You sound as if you've got it all planned out.'

Jack shrugged. 'Pretty much.'

'So how long have you been thinking about it?'

Jack grimaced. If she only knew! But all he said was, 'I haven't spent any time thinking about it. Like I said, it was a snap decision. And it's not as if you'll miss me while I'm away.'

Rachel stared at him. 'What do you want me to say, Jack?'

'Nothing.' Jack hurriedly backtracked from another confrontation. He half turned away. 'I just thought I ought to let you know what I'm doing.'

Rachel hesitated. 'What about Karen?'

'Karen!' Jack blinked at her. 'This has nothing to do with Karen.'

'Doesn't it?' Now she'd started, Rachel felt compelled to pursue it. 'Are you sure you're not just running away from a difficult situation?'

'God!' Jack gasped. 'Is that what you really think?'

'I don't know.' Rachel didn't honestly know *what* she

thought, but she couldn't believe this decision to take a month's sabbatical was motivated by overwork and nothing else. 'It just seems too—too convenient, somehow.'

'Convenient!' Jack would have liked to tell her exactly how *in*convenient his heart condition was. 'Do you really believe I'd let that—woman dictate my actions?' He scoffed. 'Think again, Rachel.'

'Well, all right. But what do you think she'll do when she finds you've left the country?'

'Left the country?' he echoed harshly. 'You make it sound as if I'm running out on her, or something. I don't care what she does, Rachel. But it seems obvious to me that you do. That even after everything I've said you still believe the kid she's carrying is mine.'

Rachel caught her breath. 'So she *is* having a baby?'

God! Jack closed his eyes for a moment, fighting for control. 'It would seem so,' he muttered at last. 'But, at the risk of becoming boring, it's not mine!'

'How do you know that?'

'What?' Jack's eyes were cold now. 'Well, duh—I think I'd remember if I'd slept with her.'

'No, I meant why are you so certain that she's not lying? How do you know she's not making it up?'

Jack wiped the back of his hand across his sweating brow. 'She sent me the result of a pregnancy test she'd taken,' he admitted wearily, deciding there was no point in holding back. 'Okay?'

'No, it's not okay.' Rachel was incensed by his attitude. 'When did she sent you this—this report?'

'A couple of days ago, I guess. Does it matter?'

'It matters to me if she's sending my husband information about a situation he denies having any responsibility for,' retorted Rachel hotly. 'What did you do with it?'

Jack sighed. 'I shredded it.' He paused. 'And forgive me if I find your indignation on my behalf rather hard to stomach. Until a few weeks ago you'd virtually forgotten you had a husband.'

'I've never forgotten,' protested Rachel, the suspicion that what had happened between them *did* form a large part of Jack's desire to get away making her step nervously towards him. 'You do believe me, don't you?' She put out a hand and touched his bare arm where the sleeve of his shirt had been turned back to his elbow. 'I wouldn't like you to—to forget it.'

'While I'm in Ireland, you mean?' Despite the fact that the brush of those sensuous fingers was causing all the blood in his veins to rush to his groin, Jack refused to let her have the upper hand. 'What are you afraid of, Rachel? That I'll find some pretty Irish colleen and slake my animal lusts with her?'

'Don't be crude!'

Rachel would have withdrawn her hand at once, but now Jack captured her wrist and prevented her from moving away. 'What's the matter?' he mocked, his green eyes narrowed between their screen of long black lashes. 'Did I prick a nerve?'

'No!'

'No?' He brought her wrist to his lips, his tongue caressing the fine tracery of veins on the inner side of her arm. 'You're a terrible liar, Rachel.'

'Unlike you,' she retorted, snatching her wrist away. 'I don't know why I believe a word you say.'

Jack arched a satirical brow. 'So,' he murmured, as if she hadn't spoken, 'will you miss me?'

'Why should I?' she demanded. 'Like you said, it's a long time since you behaved like a husband.'

Jack growled. 'I believe what I said was that you'd for-gotten you had a husband,' he reminded her harshly, once again aware of his rising pulse-rate. 'But if you want to re-sume normal sexual relations, we can talk about it when I get back.'

Rachel's jaw dropped. 'You are so full of—'

'Yeah, I know what I'm full of.'

'I was going to say *yourself,*' Rachel corrected him tremulously. 'You really believe the world revolves around Jack Riordan and no one else.'

'That's me.' Jack knew he couldn't allow himself to get involved in some explosive confrontation, and he turned towards the door again. 'Will I see you at supper?'

Rachel came after him. 'Is that all you're going to say?' she exclaimed. 'You come here and tell me you're leaving for Ireland at the end of the week, and then complicate matters by informing me that the woman who apparently thinks she has some claim on you is sending you medical reports about a baby you say you know nothing about—'

'I don't.'

'Well—' Rachel strove for a reason to keep him there. 'What am I supposed to do if she comes looking for you?'

'She won't.'

'How can you be sure?'

Jack groaned. This was getting far too heavy, far too emotional. 'I'll speak to her before I leave. I'll tell her what I'm doing—'

'Don't you dare!' The words rushed out before she could stop them. 'Don't you dare go near that woman, Jack, or—or I'll never speak to you again.'

The vulnerability of what she was saying caused Jack to hesitate. He knew this wasn't the place—and definitely not the time—for him to consider what he was thinking, but he couldn't help it. He knew it was insane, he knew he would most probably regret it, but she ignited a need in him that was virtually impossible to resist.

'You are one crazy woman,' he muttered, dropping his jacket on the floor and sliding his fingers into her hair. Then, backing her up against the bench where she stored all her painting equipment, he bent his head towards her, ignoring the warnings he'd been given and falling headlong into the sensual hunger of her kiss.

Her lips opened beneath his and he didn't hesitate before pushing his tongue into her mouth. Her hands came up to cup his face, stroking the evening roughness of his jawline before curling possessively into the longer hair at his nape.

She didn't stop him when he thrust his thigh between her legs, didn't object when he slipped his hands beneath the thin chiffon of her camisole top. She wasn't wearing a bra for working, and her breasts were warm and deliciously aroused against his hot palms. He pushed the camisole up and exposed them to his burning gaze, before lowering his head still further and taking one swollen nipple into his mouth.

His tongue circled it, caressed it, suckled on it until Rachel felt a gushing wetness between her legs. Dear God, nobody could make her feel like Jack made her feel. And although common sense warred with the desire to give in to him, sensibility and reason were fighting a losing battle.

The intense need he was generating made her want to slip out of her shorts, tear off her panties, and bare herself for him. Already she could feel his erection straining against his zipper, and the idea of making love here, in her studio, where anyone might see them, was both daring and shamefully exciting.

His hands had already slipped into her waistband, long fingers curving possessively over her bottom, giving her untold pleasure, when they were interrupted. The sound of someone clearing their throat behind them was like suddenly being plunged into a cold bath. Jack swore, but immediately pulled her camisole into place and moved away from her, pressing his stomach against the bench beside her as if he wasn't yet prepared to expose himself to anyone else's gaze.

'I—er—I'm sorry to disturb you, Mrs Riordan.' It was Mrs Grady, as Rachel had already guessed, standing some way away but within speaking distance. 'I'm afraid there's a phone call for Mr Riordan. I told her you were busy, but—well, she insisted it was urgent. I'm sorry, but what could I—'

'Did you say *she*?'

Rachel wasn't interested in Mrs Grady's apologies, and Jack knew an overwhelming sense of defeat. He was already fighting the dual demons of frustration and shortage of breath, but somehow he found the strength to turn and face them both.

'I'll take it, Mrs Grady,' he said wearily, knowing exactly who it must be. He pushed himself away from the bench and straightened up. 'In the den?'

But Rachel wasn't prepared to make it that easy for him. 'Who is it, Mrs Grady?' she asked, even though Jack guessed she was as sure of the caller's identity as he was.

'It's that Miss Johnson,' replied the housekeeper apologetically, as Jack shook his head and strode somewhat unsteadily towards the house. 'I don't know what she's doing, calling here. If it's something to do with business she should confine herself to office hours.'

CHAPTER EIGHT

'I HAVE TO go up to London on Tuesday. Why don't you come with me?'

Lucy issued the invitation on Monday morning, a week after Jack had left for Ireland, when Rachel was feeling particularly low. She'd called at the house because Rachel had told Mrs Grady she wasn't accepting any phone calls, except from her publisher, and Lucy hadn't spoken to her since the morning after they'd gone out for dinner.

Naturally she asked how things were with Jack, and Rachel had to admit that he'd gone away for a couple of weeks. She hadn't wanted to talk about it, hadn't wanted to talk about anything since Jack had left. But she should have known that Lucy would soon worm the truth out of her.

'Why?' she asked at once—a perfectly reasonable question—and Rachel was obliged to explain that he'd felt he'd needed a break.

'He's been working almost non-stop since Daddy died,' she continued hurriedly. 'And he has been looking really tired in recent weeks.'

'So why haven't you gone with him?'

'I don't have the time,' said Rachel quickly, refusing to

say he hadn't asked her. 'Besides, he's staying with his parents, and I'm not exactly their favourite daughter-in-law.'

'Because you haven't produced a baby every year?' Lucy was contemptuous. 'My God, it's medieval! The Riordans are living in the past.'

'Whatever.'

That was one subject Rachel wasn't prepared to get into. She was still too raw from what she'd learned before Jack went away. However she tried to dismiss it, she couldn't ignore the fact that Karen Johnson *was* pregnant, that she'd sent undisputed proof of her condition to Rachel's husband. And if Jack wasn't the baby's father, who was?

It hadn't helped that after the phone call that had interrupted them Jack had refused to tell her what Karen wanted. Of course Rachel's attitude hadn't helped either. She acknowledged that now. She'd been indignant, edgy, full of resentment at the way Jack had abandoned her to go and speak to the woman. That he hadn't had much choice, that asking Mrs Grady to make some excuse would have been cowardly, had only occurred to her later. As it was, her reaction had soured the situation. Jack had again accused her of not trusting him, and instead of alleviating her fears he'd told her to believe what the hell she liked.

And that was how they'd left it. Jack had spent the days before his departure organising his affairs at the office, staying away from the house whenever possible, avoiding any opportunity for another argument. Rachel didn't know if he'd seen Karen, if he'd told her what he was doing, but in any case she'd taken no chances and had refused to take any calls now he was gone.

It was hardly an ideal situation, but she was reluctant to confide that to Lucy. Besides, despite Jack's behaviour, she wasn't totally convinced he was guilty as charged. Okay, he'd known Karen for some time, and on at least one occasion he'd taken her to dinner and then spent the night at her house. But it could have been totally innocent. So why had he never mentioned the incident to her?

Of course he hadn't known she was checking up on him. He hadn't known that when he'd suggested buying the Plymouth apartment she'd become suspicious of his motives. With Lucy's help she'd had a private investigator tail him for several weeks afterwards. The fact that he'd only been seen entering the apartment with Karen on one occasion was hardly conclusive. But she'd eventually terminated the investigation and assured Lucy that she would deal with it in her own way.

'What's wrong?'

Lucy had picked up on her drifting concentration, and Rachel made a gesture of apology. 'Nothing,' she said. 'I was miles away. What were you saying?'

Lucy frowned. 'Well, I was suggesting that we could spend a couple of days in town,' she said after a moment. 'Why shouldn't you have a break, too?'

The idea was attractive, but Rachel had already insisted she was too busy to go away. A fact she was sure Lucy was perfectly well aware of. 'I wish I could,' she said now, turning to the tray that Mrs Grady had set on the table beside her chair. 'Iced tea? With lemon or without?'

'With.' Lucy tilted her face to the sun. They were sitting outside on the patio, and the early cloud cover was giving way to another hot day. 'Mmm, this is nice, isn't it? Who needs a holiday when you live here?'

It was another dig at Jack, but Rachel chose to ignore it. 'I like it,' she said instead. Then, forcing an optimism she didn't feel, 'So, why have you got to go to London? Are you staying overnight?'

'Like I say, I may stay a few days,' said Lucy, her tone saying she was aware of Rachel's attempt at distracting her. 'In any case, it's just business.' She glanced back at the big house. 'Don't you find it lonely here, all on your own?'

'I have Mrs Grady,' replied Rachel, lifting her glass of tea to her lips.

'She's your housekeeper!' exclaimed Lucy. 'She's hardly a friend.'

'Oh, Mrs Grady is good company,' Rachel insisted. 'She and I get on together really well.'

Lucy shook her head. 'And you're prepared to stay here, like the good little wife you are, until Jack chooses to come back, right?'

Rachel sighed. 'It's not like that, Lucy. If—if I wanted to go to Ireland I'd go. But I don't.'

'You *are* sure he's gone on his own, I suppose?'

Rachel stared at her. 'Of course.'

'You only have his word for it, though, don't you?'

'Lucy, he's gone to stay at his parents' house. Don't you think they'd have something to say if he took a—another woman there?'

Lucy shrugged. 'Maybe.'

'What's that supposed to mean?'

'Well…' Lucy considered. 'It's possible that the Riordans wouldn't have too many objections if Jack divorced you and married someone else.'

'Lucy, the Riordans are staunch Catholics. One of Jack's brothers is a priest. They don't believe in divorce.'

'Well, that's their story.' But Lucy didn't sound convinced. 'And if it meant that Jack could provide them with a handful of little Riordans…'

'Don't go there, Lucy.' Rachel was on her feet before the other woman had finished speaking. Crossing the patio, she gripped the boundary wall with grim hands. Then, with her back to Lucy, she said, 'I think you'd better go. Before I say something we'd both regret.'

'Oh, Rachel.' She heard Lucy get to her feet and cross the tiled expanse to join her. 'That was tactless. And cruel, I know. I'm sorry. But I am only thinking of you. Surely you know that?'

'Do I?' Rachel stared out at the beauty of Foliot Cove, wondering why it gave her so little pleasure at this moment. 'I think you intended to hurt me, Lucy—'

'No!'

'—and you did. Please go.'

'Rachel.' Lucy put tentative fingers on her shoulder. 'Darling, don't be like this. We've been friends for too long. Don't let Jack Riordan come between us.'

'Jack Riordan is my husband.' Rachel moved away from her hand and turned to face her. 'I know you feel bitter because of the way Martin treated you, but Jack's not like that.'

Lucy regarded her with guarded eyes. 'You don't think?'

'I know,' said Rachel, though she was lying even to herself. What did she really know—except that Karen Johnson was pregnant? Jack had insisted it wasn't his baby, and she wanted to believe him. But he *would* deny it, wouldn't he? Even if it was true. 'I don't want to talk about it any more.'

'Then we won't.' Lucy saw a chance to redeem herself and took it. 'Darling, come and sit down again. Let's enjoy our tea together. Did I tell you I saw Claire Stanford last week? She's put on such a lot of weight I hardly recognised her.'

In spite of her misgivings, Rachel let Lucy coax her back to the lounge chairs. She was probably a fool for giving in, she thought, but Lucy was her closest friend—and who else did she have to talk to? Besides, Lucy might be right. Maybe the Riordans *would* be prepared to compromise their beliefs if they thought it would make Jack happy. It wasn't something she wanted to think about, and she'd certainly never admit as much to her friend. But the seed had been sown and it took root.

It was so quiet.

Even after three weeks at Ballyryan, Jack still hadn't got used to the absence of cars and traffic jams, of planes flying overhead, of raised voices and the constant sound of phones ringing somewhere in the building.

When he'd first arrived, he used to wake in the middle of the night with his heart hammering, his pulses racing, and his nerves as tight as violin strings. He'd spend the next half-hour straining to hear what had woken him. It had taken him a week to realise it was the silence, the absolute lack of any noise whatsoever, that had disturbed him. In its own way it was deafening, like the sudden pounding of a drum.

He was used to that now, though, used—most nights anyway—to sleeping eight or nine hours at a stretch. No one disturbed him. No one brought him early-morning cups of tea or coffee unless he asked for it. His parents went about their daily lives without asking him a lot of unnecessary questions. They were there if he needed them, but otherwise they gave him all the time and space he wished for.

Nor did they treat him like an invalid, even though Jack had been forced to tell them what his doctor had said. He doubted they'd even heard of arrhythmia until he'd described it to them, and, although his mother hadn't been able to hide her anxiety at first, she was dealing with it.

A tug on the line Jack had extended into Lough Ryan alerted him to the fact that something was biting. His father was a keen fisherman, and in recent days Jack, too, had discovered the pleasures of just sitting on the bank of the small lake and letting time glide by. His parents' cottage overlooked the lough, so he didn't have far to go. Carrying a folded canvas chair and a striped umbrella—because County Wexford wasn't so green by accident—he'd set himself up with his rod and a flask of iced water, and drift on the soft, scented air.

The catch proved to be too small to bother with and, releasing it, Jack let the quivering fish slide back into the water. It splashed for a moment in the reeds before gliding swiftly away, and Jack resumed his lazy contemplation of the shoreline opposite.

He wondered if fishing made Jude Riordan such a laid-back character. Yet, despite making light of his wife's fears, his father had instigated a distinctly more in-depth discussion with his son when Maggie wasn't around. In his opinion, Jack's problem was a pain in the ass, no doubt about it. But, as the doctors had said, the solution was in his own hands.

His actual words had been that Jack should stop mucking around before he did something really stupid like killing himself. And, although he was sure the Blessed Virgin would be pleased to see Jack, he'd prefer it if it wasn't quite yet.

It was that kind of simple logic that Jack appreciated. The old man usually talked good sense, even if Jack didn't always take his advice. And if Jude suspected Rachel might be partly to blame for some of the stress his son was suffering, he didn't say it. And Jack was too proud to explain why his relationship with his wife was falling apart.

All the same, Jack had been relieved when he'd learned of the specialists' findings. There didn't appear to be anything wrong with him that couldn't be cured with drugs and a change in his lifestyle. Diet, a limited intake of caffeine, and no alcohol for starters, together with more exercise and food at regular times.

According to Dr Moore, his condition wasn't uncommon. Many men in his position never considered their health until it was too late. And the truth was, although he'd told Rachel he needed a month or six weeks' break, he'd been advised to take six *months* away from the office. But then, Dr Moore thought his relationship with his wife was solid. He had no idea what was going on in Jack's life.

'Jack! Jack!'

The sound of his mother calling his name brought an abrupt return to reality. With definite reluctance, Jack secured the umbrella and got up from his chair. It was too early for lunch, and he couldn't imagine what had put that note of urgency into her voice.

By the time he'd turned to climb the slight rise between the lakeshore and the cottage, Maggie Riordan was standing on the ridge looking down at him. A slim, attractive woman in her fifties, with hair that had once been as dark and glossy as her son's, she had her arms wrapped around her waist and there was a definite look of concern on her face.

She held out a hand to help Jack up the steepest part of the climb, but her son just gave her an old-fashioned look. 'Yeah, make me feel like a real wuss, why don't you?' he muttered drily, taking a deep breath before making the final step to bring him level. 'So—where's the fire?'

Maggie balled a fist and pushed it playfully against his

chest. 'No fire,' she said, looking up into his dark face with warm, loving eyes. She glanced back towards the cottage, as if to assure herself that she hadn't been followed. 'You've got a visitor.'

Jack's heart raced and his stomach muscles tightened. For a crazy moment he wondered if it could be Rachel. He missed her so much. But common sense soon kicked in. For one thing his mother would have said that *Rachel* was here, not just that he had *a visitor*.

'Who is it?' he asked. Then his shoulders sagged as another thought occurred to him. 'Not Father Patrick!'

'No, it's not Father Patrick,' retorted his mother sharply. 'Not that you wouldn't do well to pay more attention to what he has to say. Just because you've been living in that heathen country all these years doesn't mean you should neglect your faith, Jack.'

Faith! Jack grimaced. But all he said was, 'England's not a heathen country, Ma. You lived there long enough yourself. For pity's sake, I was born there.'

'You're still of good Irish stock,' Maggie declared firmly. 'Now, before you go and greet your visitor, is there anything you'd like to tell me?'

Jack stared at her. 'Like what?'

'You've got nothing on your conscience, then?'

'On my conscience?' Despite the progress he'd made, Jack could feel his mother's words getting to him. 'What the hell is this all about?'

'There's no need for that language, Jack.' Maggie looked offended. 'Sure you'd better come and see for yourself. It isn't fair to keep the young woman waiting. Not when she's come such a long way to see you.'

'Wait.' Jack dug his heels into the soft turf and didn't move. 'Did you say "young woman"?'

'There's nothing wrong with your hearing, Jack.' Maggie regarded him reprovingly. 'Are you saying that's jogged your memory?'

Jack scowled. 'I don't believe it!'

'What don't you believe?' His mother frowned. 'She's here. You can believe that. And she's quite obviously going to have a baby. You can believe that, too. Is it yours?'

'No!'

Jack groaned. He told himself this couldn't be happening, but it was. Karen was here. Somehow she'd found out where his parents lived and she'd followed him. It had taken her over three weeks, maybe, but he knew only too well how determined she could be.

'All right.' For now, at least, his mother had accepted his word, but how long would that last once Karen started spinning her lies? 'Well, as I say,' she continued, 'best not keep her waiting, hmm?'

Jack pulled in a long breath, dragging much needed air into his lungs. He was trying not to let this psyche him, but the knowledge that Karen was actually here, in Ballyryan, was a bitter reality. What did she want here? What was she trying to do to him? She couldn't prove it was his baby. But the damnable thing was he couldn't prove that it wasn't.

Not yet.

Karen was waiting for him in the neat whitewashed parlour of the cottage. Like many of their neighbours, the Riordans only used the parlour on special occasions, and it annoyed the hell out of Jack that Karen should be here, polluting the atmosphere of his parents' home.

She rose to her feet as he came in, and the first thing he noticed was that the pregnancy was far more advanced than he'd expected. But then it was months since he'd seen her, and what did he know about it anyway?

'Hello, Jack,' she said, the simpering tone of her voice really grating on him. She was wearing a pink-flowered halter-necked dress that was pulled taut over her full breasts and bulging stomach. 'I hope you don't mind me coming here, but I really had to see you.'

'Why?' Ignoring his mother's sudden intake of breath, Jack propped his shoulder against the doorjamb and regarded her with cold eyes. 'What do you want?'

'Jack!'

It was his mother who made the shocked exclamation, but Jack didn't look at her. 'Well?' he said, still staring at Karen. 'What do you want? I thought I made my position clear before I left England.'

'Oh, Jack!' Karen fumbled in her bag for a tissue. Then, simulating tears, she pressed the tissue to her eyes. 'Don't be like this. You know I love you.'

Jack turned angry eyes in his mother's direction, not at all surprised to see the horror on her face. Karen could be so damn convincing. Didn't he know it?

Struggling with a threatening sense of panic, Jack fought for control. 'This isn't going to work, Karen,' he said grimly. 'I suggest you stop wasting your time and mine and get the hell out of here.'

'Oh, Jack.' Once again Karen dissolved into tears, sinking back into the armchair where she'd been sitting and burying her face in her hands. 'How can you be so cruel? After everything we've been to one another.'

Jack couldn't take any more of this. Pushing past his mother, he groped his way outside, standing with his shoulders pressed against the walls of the cottage until his heartbeat slowed to a steadier beat.

He was still standing there, with his eyes closed against the pitiless glare of the sun, when he heard the approach of footsteps. For a moment he was disoriented, the sound was coming from the opposite direction than he'd expected. But it was definitely a woman's footsteps, and when he opened his eyes he found Rachel was there, staring at him with a look of real anxiety on her face.

CHAPTER NINE

JACK WONDERED IF he should add hallucination to his list of ailments. Maybe the fact that the hot sun had been burning his eyelids was responsible for him seeing Rachel standing motionless now on the path that led up to the door. She couldn't be here, not today of all days, not with Karen holding court in his mother's parlour. However much he'd longed to see her, it had to be some kind of sick joke.

But then she spoke, and Jack knew both his greatest wish and his greatest fear had collided.

'Jack!' she exclaimed, abandoning her stance and hurrying towards him. She laid a soft, cool hand on his forehead. 'Jack, what's wrong? You look—ill!'

And he did, Rachel thought, realising she'd dismissed his need for a break too casually. She should have known it wasn't like him to abandon his responsibilities, to leave the running of the company to someone else, unless he had to. It was obvious he'd needed more than a holiday, and she hadn't recognised that.

Jack closed his eyes for a moment, still half hoping he was imagining it. But when she squeezed his wrist he knew there was no escape. 'I—I was a little hot, that's all,' he said, knowing that once Rachel found out that Karen was here she'd think she'd found the reason for his agitation. 'Um…' He swallowed. 'How did you get here?'

'The usual way.' Right now, Rachel wasn't interested in explaining the route she'd taken. 'I flew to Dublin and caught a train to Wexford.' She shrugged. 'Does it matter? I'm here now.' She looked up into his face with wide searching eyes. 'Are you glad to see me?'

Jack groaned. 'Yes.'

A relieved smile touched her lips. 'I didn't know if you would be,' she confessed. 'After the way I behaved before you left.' She shook her head. 'I'm such a fool sometimes.'

Jack wet his lips. 'That makes two of us.'

'So why didn't you tell me?'

'Tell you what?' For a moment Jack thought Dr Moore had been talking, but then he realised it was more than the doctor's job was worth to divulge a patient's medical details—even to his wife. 'If you mean the fact that I've been—feeling out of sorts, I *did* tell you.'

'Yes, but I thought—' She broke off. What had she thought? Rachel wondered unhappily. She been so strung up with this business over Karen Johnson she'd thought he was stringing her a line. 'Anyway, it's obvious it was more serious than I imagined.'

'I look that bad, huh?'

'No. Yes.' Rachel made a helpless gesture. 'It's not that. You look a little pale, yes, and I realise you must have felt pretty bad to leave your job. But it wasn't until I spoke to George that I realised I was partly to blame.'

Jack stared at her. 'You've been talking to George? George Thomas?'

'Who else? I don't know any other Georges,' said Rachel soothingly. 'Now, don't look like that. He's concerned about you, too. And when he said you were having—personal problems, well—I knew he had to mean me.'

Jack blinked. 'Is that all he said?'

'Pretty much.' Rachel moved a little nearer. 'Oh, God, Jack, I have missed you.'

'Have you?'

It was what he'd most wanted to hear. That she'd actually made this journey because she cared about him. Okay, maybe she felt a little sorry for him, too, but it wasn't pity he could see in her luminous blue eyes.

And at any other time…

'Do you want me to prove it?'

Rachel had no idea what he was thinking. She was tilting her head, allowing her fingers to play with the hairs on his wrist. In a short black skirt that flared about her thighs, and a cream lace cardigan whose buttons ended some inches above her bare midriff, she was more beautiful than ever. And so sexy that Jack felt the familiar tug of longing in his gut.

As if she'd sensed what he was thinking, she glanced about her. 'Where are Maggie and Jude?' she asked. 'I suppose I ought to let them know I'm here.' Her knee nudged his. 'Unless we've got the place to ourselves?'

Jack expelled an uneven breath. Her words reminded him of where they were, and he prayed the sound of her voice hadn't carried into the cottage. 'They're not here,' he lied, knowing that whatever happened afterwards he needed this time alone with her. And, when she would have drawn him towards the door, he slipped his hand about her waist. 'Let's not go into the house. It's too nice a day to be inside.'

'If you say so.' The tip of her tongue appeared, to moisten her upper lip. 'Where shall we go?'

'Leave that to me,' muttered Jack, coming to a decision. Taking her hand, he practically dragged her around the side of the cottage to where the Aston Martin was parked. For the first time since his arrival he was glad he'd chosen to make the sea crossing so that he could bring his car with him, and, hauling open the passenger side door, he ushered Rachel inside.

'Don't you need keys?' she ventured, when he rounded the car and coiled his length behind the wheel. Her eyes danced. 'Or do the fairies start the engine for you?'

'Something like that,' he agreed, showing her the keys, already in the ignition. 'No one locks their car in Ballyryan. Sure, and don't the saints themselves keep an eye on them for us?'

Rachel giggled, a wonderful gurgle of laughter that Jack hadn't heard for far too long. Unable to resist touching her, as if he still couldn't quite believe she was real, he stretched out his arm and gripped her thigh just above her knee. His fingers curled into her soft flesh with a tensile pleasure, feeling the way she moved to make it easier for him.

He wanted to continue. The temptation to slide his hand up her leg, under the short hem of her skirt, was almost irresistible. The way she'd reacted, he was sure she'd be hot and ready for him, and he would have liked nothing better than to have the smell and the taste of her on his fingertips.

But he knew better than to take that risk. It was only a matter of time before his mother got impatient and came looking for him. Obviously she'd seen his distress, and she was prepared to give him a breathing space. But after the way Karen had behaved she would expect an explanation. Even if, like Rachel, she was unlikely to believe it.

Starting the car before the encroaching cloud of despair could descend upon him, he thrust the lever into 'drive' and pulled away from the cottage. Thankfully, although it had rained in the night, the ground beneath the Aston Martin was dry, and there wasn't the sound of skidding tyres to give him away.

Once they were a safe distance from his parents' home, Jack rolled down the windows and took a gulp of clean country air. God, in spite of everything it was so good to be feeling half human again, he thought. He wouldn't think about Karen—wouldn't think about what Rachel might say when she saw her. For now, they were alone in a painted landscape, with the grey-green waters of Lough Ryan on one side and the rugged slopes of a river valley on the other.

They'd turned off the major road and this track was virtually deserted. Occasionally they'd glimpse a tractor toiling across a field, or a horse-drawn cart, but tourists usually kept to more familiar routes. Once they did see an optimistic traveller pulling a caravan, and here and there an isolated cottage broke the view. But for the most part they had the scenery to themselves.

'Mmm, this is heavenly,' Rachel murmured, putting her hands behind her head and giving a contented sigh. 'I'm so glad I came.'

Jack frowned. 'Where are your bags?' he asked, realising she hadn't brought a suitcase. He nodded to the suede pouch she'd tossed onto the back seat. 'Surely you can't have everything you need in there?'

'Perhaps I do.' Rachel gave another gurgle of laughter. She kicked off one of her sling-backed sandals to draw up her knee and rest her heel on the soft leather of her seat. 'A change of underwear, at least.'

'And the rest?' enquired Jack drily, recalling how many suitcases she'd always taken when they'd gone on holiday together. 'Come on, baby. This is me you're talking to, remember?'

'I know.' Rachel gave him a sideways look. She was loath to admit she'd spent last night at a hotel in Dublin. But, dammit, it had taken some courage to buy a ticket to Wexford this morning. She hadn't known how Jack would react when he saw her. 'They're at the hotel.'

'What hotel?'

'The Gresham,' she admitted reluctantly, mentioning the name of one of Dublin's oldest and finest hostelries. 'I—I didn't know if you'd want me to stay.'

'Right.'

Jack blew out a breath. It wasn't such a leap, he knew. They hadn't exactly parted on the best of terms. He hadn't even made an attempt to contact her since he'd got here, and even now he wasn't absolutely sure what she really wanted of him.

Rachel turned, one knee coiled beneath her now, her arm along the back of his seat. 'You're not mad at me, are you?' she whispered, her fingers grazing his ear, causing goosebumps on the nape of his neck. 'These last three weeks have been the longest of my life.'

'Don't be stupid,' he said hoarsely, his hands tightening on the wheel. Then, finding what he was looking for, he swung the car through a break in the hedge and they bumped down a narrow gully. He stopped the car halfway down, turned off the engine and held out his hand. 'Come on,' he urged, opening his door. 'There's something I want you to see.'

Rachel grabbed her sandals off the floor and scrambled over the central console. She paused a moment, turning sideways on his seat to put her sandals on again, and then stood up, wobbling a little on the high heels. 'Where are we?'

'If you come with me, I'll show you,' replied Jack, deliberately mysterious. He reached for her hand and paused a moment, looking down at her. Then he bent and took her mouth in a hot searching kiss before starting down the track again, Rachel struggling to keep her balance and her head.

'Wait,' she said after a moment, pulling her hand free to support herself against the rough bole of a pine tree. She kicked off her sandals and pulled a face. 'You'll have to carry me if it gets too rough.'

'I guess I could,' agreed Jack drily, already imagining how delightful that would be. Then he shook his head. 'But don't worry. It's not far now.'

The final part of the slope led through a grove of trees. Rachel was unaware of what she was going to see until they emerged on a mossy plateau above a pool that reflected the clear blue of the sky overhead.

The rocky shelf hugged the bank of the pool, and their arrival caused a flock of ducks to flutter in panic out of the reeds. At the other side of the pool, more trees formed a natural windbreak, and half hidden by a fold in the hillside the ruins of what might once have been a church or an abbey gave the lush valley an air of haunting isolation.

'It's beautiful!' Gazing about her, Rachel was enchanted by her surroundings. 'What is this place? How did you know it was here?'

'It's called St. Michael's Pool,' replied Jack, leaving her to squat at the water's edge. 'In the days when the monastery was still in use, I imagine the monks used this pool for just about everything: drinking, washing, irrigating their crops. I believe they were pretty self-sufficient.'

Rachel went to join him. 'That was a monastery?'

She stared at the uneven piles of grey stone. 'It must be very old.'

'Several hundred years, at least,' agreed Jack, straightening and tossing the pebble he'd found into the pool. The ripples spread and he watched them. Then he went on, 'The water here is as clear and as cold as ice. It's supposed to well up from some underground spring, but my brothers and I could never find it.'

Rachel's eyes went wide. 'You used to swim here?'

'When we were kids.' Jack nodded, bending to pull out one of the reeds and twisting it between his strong fingers. 'My grandparents lived at Ballyryan when we were young, and they used to have us all to stay in the long summer holidays.'

'But this place is miles from Ballyryan.'

Jack grinned a little ruefully. 'We had bikes. We used to ride for miles. Gran and Grandpa didn't know where we were half the time.' His grin deepened. 'We loved it.'

'I bet you did.' It was very warm in the enclosed valley, but Rachel shivered. 'Jack, this pool looks awfully deep. You could have drowned.'

'You don't think about things like that when you're a kid,' said Jack carelessly. 'Besides, we were all fairly good swimmers. Even my sisters. It was an adventure.' He paused. 'D'you want to try it?'

Rachel caught her breath and automatically took a step backwards. 'Swim in the pool, you mean?'

He shrugged. 'If you dare.'

Rachel shook her head. 'It's not a question of daring,' she said, dry-mouthed at the prospect. 'You've said yourself, kids come here. What if someone saw us?'

Jack didn't say anything. He just tossed the reed aside and hauled his tee shirt over his head—and Rachel's knees went weak at the sight of his broad muscled frame. It was crazy. He was her husband, for God's sake. But the prospect of getting naked with him here was as tempting and provocative as if they were teenagers.

Her fingers went automatically to the buttons of her cardigan. 'I—we'd be in the water, wouldn't we?' she probed. 'If anyone did come around.'

'Initially,' said Jack, feeling the semi-arousal he'd had since seeing Rachel again hardening into a rigid erection. 'Unless you have a better idea?'

Rachel quivered, but without further hesitation she unbuttoned her cardigan and peeled it off her sweating shoulders. The pool did look very inviting, and in her present state of sexual intoxication it would be good to cool off.

Or would it? Watching Jack unzipping his pants, pushing the jeans down his strong legs, revealing that he wasn't wearing any underwear, did crazy things to her equilibrium. He was half turned away from her, but that didn't prevent her from seeing his shaft rising proudly from its nest of dark hair. If she'd had any doubts that he wanted her they were instantly dispelled, and the urge to go to him and press herself against his aroused body was a disturbing temptation.

But then it wasn't. Jack took the uncertainty out of her hands by diving headfirst into the pool, He made a huge splash, and the water he displaced flooded over Rachel's bare feet. She hopped from foot to foot as the wave receded. Damn, that was cold. There couldn't be much wrong with Jack if he could stand this.

He came up, swiping his wet hair out of his eyes, looking like some pagan god bathing in the pool. 'What are you waiting for?' he asked mockingly. 'Are you chicken?'

Rachel took only a moment before unfastening her skirt

and stepping out of it. She laid it out of reach of the water, and without removing her underwear stepped to the water's edge. Then, closing her eyes and offering a prayer that she wouldn't make a fool of herself, she gripped her nose and jumped into the pool.

She seemed to go down forever before the buoyancy of her body brought her back to the surface. She came up gasping, as much with the cold as with a shortage of air. God, the water was freezing, she thought. It had to be only a few degrees above freezing point. It was like swimming in the Antarctic. She wouldn't have been surprised if there were penguins as well as ducks nesting in the reeds.

Jack swam towards her, grinning maliciously. 'Great, isn't it? Just what you need on a hot day.'

Rachel shuddered, only just stopping her teeth from chattering. 'If—if you like this sort of thing,' she muttered. 'My legs feel numb.'

'That's because you're not using them,' replied Jack reasonably. 'Come on. Let's swim to the other side. You'll feel warmer once you're moving.'

'You think?'

Rachel wasn't convinced, but Jack merely shook his head and, kicking his legs, swam powerfully across the pool. He was completely at home in the water. Deciding she didn't have a lot of choice in the matter, Rachel filled her lungs with air and followed him.

He was right. She did feel infinitely warmer by the time she'd swum a dozen yards. Even the water didn't feel so cold any more, and she halted near him, kicking her legs and spreading her arms wide, enjoying the sensation of silky water against her skin.

'Imagine how the monks would feel if they could see

you now,' Jack teased her. 'Although I don't know why you're still wearing a bra. It's not protecting anything.'

Rachel glanced down and realised he was right. The wet lace clung to her skin, exposing the rosy globes of her breasts, accentuating the swollen peaks that pushed so aggressively against the cream silk.

'Here.' Jack moved behind her. 'Let me.' And moments later the bra floated free beside her. 'That's better,' he said huskily, moving closer to cup her breasts in his hands. 'Much better.'

Rachel gulped in anticipation, and Jack didn't disappoint her. Moving even closer, he allowed his hand to slide familiarly over her bottom, bringing her into intimate contact with his lower body. Then, using his free hand to keep them afloat, he wrapped one leg around her and stroked her parted lips with his tongue.

It was so sensuous, so erotic, Jack could feel his senses spinning in response. But it was a good feeling and, lifting his head, he said thickly, 'Let's get out of here.'

Rachel grabbed her bra and they swam back to where they'd left their clothes. Jack hauled himself out of the water and offered his hand to Rachel. She scrambled onto the plateau beside him, and before she could even take a full breath he was bearing her back against the rocks.

His kiss was hot and fierce, but also intensely sensual. Her mouth opened for him, welcomed his tongue with an urgency that had her arching up against him. He groaned, searching her mouth with a possessive hunger, and a raw shudder shook his powerful frame.

He muttered a little curse when his exploring hands encountered the strings of her bikini briefs. But in no time at all, it seemed, Rachel felt them slip away, felt the coolness of wet stone against her buttocks.

The ground was hard beneath her, but she hardly noticed when Jack moved to lie over her, his erection thrusting solidly against her stomach. His mouth trailed down her neck, nipping the soft flesh that was feathered with goosebumps, turning her warming skin a delicious shade of pink.

Jack could feel her body heating up. Cool arms tightened about his neck, nails dug painfully into his scalp, and she grabbed his face and brought his mouth back to hers. This time her tongue thrust eagerly into his mouth, and with a growl of satisfaction he muttered, 'Open your legs.'

Although her skin was cool, inside she was hot and wet, a delicious fire just waiting to burn him up. Muscles that had welcomed him several weeks ago were more than ready to accommodate him again. She took him wholly and completely, and so deep it felt as if he was touching her womb.

It was amazing how little she cared about their exposure now, thought Rachel dizzily. The idea that someone might take it into their heads to come down to the pool, might be watching them at this very minute, only added to the sense of excitement and freedom she was feeling. The knowledge that Jack was a part of her again was all that mattered to her. He felt so good inside her, so big and powerful. He filled her physically and spiritually, and she was already halfway to her first orgasm when he put his hand down between them and massaged the swollen nub hidden in the moist curls of blond hair.

'Is that good?' he asked, albeit a little hoarsely, and Rachel couldn't prevent the feelings inside her from rising to an uncontrollable crescendo. She bucked beneath him, clinging to him for dear life, and he bent to stifle her cry with his lips.

'Just in case anyone's listening,' he said softly, beginning to move again, bringing her to a second and third orgasm before he allowed his own release.

He came violently, pumping his hips against her until he was totally spent. Then he dropped his head into the hollow of her neck and knew a sense of peace and satisfaction even greater than the last time they'd made love in her bedroom.

He closed his eyes, wanting to prolong the moment, not wanting to withdraw from her quite yet. He knew if they'd been anywhere else than here he'd have made love to her again, but it wasn't fair to make her lie on the rocky ground any longer than this.

Besides, he knew they ought to get back to Ballyryan. He wasn't looking forward to it, but he couldn't put off the evil day any longer. Nevertheless, the prospect of how Rachel was going to react when she found Karen there didn't bear thinking about, and with a groan of despair he rolled onto his back.

'Are you all right, Jack?'

Almost immediately Rachel was leaning over him, concern in her troubled blue eyes, her breasts tantalisingly close to his mouth. He knew he had to do something before lust got the better of him, and, pushing himself up onto his elbows, he said softly, 'I just wish we didn't have to go back.'

'It won't be so bad.' Rachel was optimistic. 'And I can stay until Monday. That means we've got the whole weekend to ourselves—and your bed will be much more comfortable than here.'

Jack stifled a groan, wanting to tell her, to warn her of what awaited them, but he couldn't spoil her delight in the moment. 'I love you' he said. 'Never forget that.'

'And I love you, too,' she whispered in return. 'Oh, Jack, I've been such a fool.'

* * *

It was after one o'clock when they got back to the cottage. Jack had spent the journey trying to find a way to tell her about Karen, but the words just wouldn't come. How could he tell his wife that the woman who claimed to be his mistress had turned up without an invitation? If Rachel hadn't believed him before, why should he think she'd believe him now?

He parked the car in the same spot as before, but when Rachel made to get out he caught her hand. 'Wait,' he said. 'There's something I have to tell you.'

Rachel frowned, torn between the desire to get the meeting with her mother-in-law over with and the troubled look on Jack's face. She had little doubt that Maggie Riordan would have her own opinion of Rachel's behaviour, and no one could deny she hadn't been afraid to voice it in the past.

But before either of them could say anything Maggie herself appeared, coming to meet them with an unexpected smile of welcome on her face. 'Well, and there you are, Rachel,' she exclaimed. 'And didn't I see you going off with himself a couple of hours ago?' She turned to her son. 'What's going on, Jack? Sure, are you trying to keep her all to yourself?'

Jack was stunned, and, obviously understanding his confusion, his mother gave Rachel a quick hug before tucking a hand in each of their arms. 'Come along now,' she said. 'Your father and I have been waiting lunch for you. And Rachel, of course.' She gave her daughter-in-law a huge smile. 'It's so good to see you, lassie. It's about time you came and took this man of yours in hand.'

CHAPTER TEN

RACHEL FLEW BACK to London on Monday morning. Jack had driven her up to Dublin on Sunday evening, and they'd spent the night in the suite she'd expected to use during her stay. It had been a magical night, made all the more poignant by her impending departure. Rachel hadn't wanted to go, and Jack had most definitely wanted her to stay.

But she had commitments. A deadline on the book she was illustrating that couldn't be extended. And, short of terrifying her with exaggerated claims about his heart condition, Jack had had no choice than to accept her decision.

Nevertheless, he bade her goodbye in the departure lounge at the airport with a troubling feeling of apprehension. There was so much he'd wanted to tell her; so much he'd left unsaid. Although he'd been forced to admit that Dr Moore had practically ordered him to rest, he'd said nothing about the complicated tests he'd had at the clinic in Plymouth. She was still labouring under the impression that he'd be home himself in a week or so, and, despite not actually saying it, Jack had known she'd hoped he'd pack his bags and leave with her.

And he'd been tempted. Being with Rachel again was

the most important thing in his life. Only the fact that his mother had been horrified when he'd confided as much to her had persuaded him that he'd be foolish to ignore the warnings he'd been given.

Besides, after the way his mother had dealt with Karen, he felt obliged to take her advice. Instead of believing her story, Maggie had apparently told Karen in no uncertain terms that her son didn't lie, and that if he said the baby she was carrying wasn't his, it wasn't. End of story.

Naturally he hadn't heard every detail of their exchange yet. Only that after delivering her verdict his mother had arranged for McGinty's taxi to pick Karen up and take her to the station in Wexford. 'I've given her her fare back to Dublin, and that's more than she deserves,' Maggie had gone on staunchly, when her son had cornered her in the kitchen after lunch that day. 'Sure, we can't talk about this now, but rest assured I wouldn't have a besom like that in my house!'

Jack had been amazed. And grateful. 'So she went?'

'She didn't have any choice,' his mother had declared proudly. Then she'd smirked. 'Sure, I don't think you'll have any more truck with her.'

Jack wished he could believe her, but when he would have said more a sharp shake of his mother's head had warned him they were no longer alone. Rachel was behind him, standing in the doorway, her eyebrows raised enquiringly. 'Is something wrong?'

'Now, what could be wrong?' exclaimed Jack's mother, drying her hands on a tea towel. 'Jack was just telling me you're staying.'

'If that's all right.'

Maggie smiled. 'You're welcome here at any time, Rachel. You should know that.' Then, giving her son a warning look, she added, 'I gather you had a good time together this morning? Jack's a lucky man. It's to be hoped he appreciates it.'

Rachel went to tuck her hand through Jack's arm. 'I'm sure he does,' she said huskily, and no one could be in any doubt that she meant what she said.

Maggie had given her son another meaningful look, but all she'd said was, 'Well, I'm glad the two of you have finally come to your senses. Don't let anything—or anyone—come between you.'

That had been on Friday afternoon, but now, with his wife several thousand feet above the Irish Sea, Jack couldn't help wishing he'd been honest with her about Karen's visit. It was all very well his mother telling him to play it safe, but she didn't know Karen as he did. The woman was unscrupulous, totally without conscience. She seemed determined to break up his marriage, and if he had any sense he'd get back to England as soon as he could.

But when he broached that subject with his mother later that day she told him he was mad to consider it. 'Until that woman's arrival I couldn't understand why you and Rachel were still having marital problems,' she said. 'Oh, I suppose I had some notion of what the lassie must have gone through, losing three babies and all. I dare say she was afraid of getting pregnant again, even if your pa and I didn't approve of her barring you from her bed. But that was almost two years ago, and I'd have expected you to have settled your differences by now. Then, when that woman appeared on my doorstep, I realised why Rachel was still in England and you were here, on your own.'

'It's not that simple, Ma—'

'I accept that. But hear me out, Jack.' She paused. 'First of all, did you have an affair with her?'

'With Karen?' Jack snorted. 'Hell, no!'

'But Rachel thinks you did?'

'Maybe.'

'Okay.' Maggie frowned. 'So why does this woman think you are the father of her child?'

Jack shook his head. 'I don't know.'

'She says you had an affair with her,' went on his mother, more calmly that he would have expected. 'She says it started one evening when you'd had too much to drink and stayed the night.'

Jack groaned. 'I did not have too much to drink.'

'She says you said you did.'

Jack sighed. 'Okay, I did say that—yeah.' He scowled. 'But you know what was going on. I'd been feeling pretty lousy all evening, but I didn't want to admit as much to her. I don't remember exactly what happened. We were standing at her door, saying good night, and I felt really dizzy. I tried to take my pulse. You know—a surreptitious hand around the wrist. But it wasn't there. The next thing I knew, I was lying on her sofa.'

'With your clothes on?'

Jack's mouth compressed. 'Most of them.'

'What's that supposed to mean?'

His colour deepened. 'It means she'd taken off my jacket and loosened my collar.'

'How about your trousers?'

'I was still wearing my pants,' protested Jack indignantly. 'My God, Ma, what are you getting at? That I had sex with her and didn't know it?'

Maggie arched her dark brows. 'Is it possible?'

'No.' Jack scowled. 'For pity's sake, I thought you believed me.'

'I do believe you,' she said placidly. 'But there's no point in denying that I'd like to know all the facts.'

'Okay.'

'So why did you go out with her?' His mother looked disapproving now. 'Jack, you're a married man. What were you thinking, going out with a woman like that?'

'It was only one time,' said Jack defensively. 'You have to remember, I was feeling pretty low. Rachel and I—well, we seemed to have lost touch with one another. That was part of the problem, I guess. I was working every hour God sent, and I needed someone to talk to.'

'But why her?'

'I don't know. Because she was available, I suppose. Looking back on it now, I realise that she was always hanging about Myrna's office. I used to think she and Myrna were friends, but it was obviously me she was hoping to see.'

'So you what? Took her out to dinner?'

'Yeah. And all this harassment—the stalking, the phone calls—they all stem from that one evening.'

'She says you fired her because you were tired of her.'

Jack groaned. 'Just for the record, I didn't fire her. That was George. She worked in George's office, not mine. And he said she was useless at her job.'

'And after she was fired she started pestering you.'

Jack gave a short mirthless laugh. *'Pestering?'* he echoed. 'It was a bit more than that. Until I got Harry to move her on, she used to stake out the car park. She knew what time I usually left in the evenings, and she'd be waiting for me.'

'But why you? Why not George Thomas?'

'Because he hadn't been foolish enough to take her out, I suppose. She used to tell me how much she missed the office, that she was miserable because she couldn't get another job. I felt sorry for her, but I didn't do or say anything to encourage her to think that I wanted to see her again. Then, when cajoling didn't work, she started threatening me. She said if I didn't agree to see her, she'd tell Rachel we'd been having an affair.'

'Oh, Jack!'

'She didn't. Not then, anyway. And I thought she was bluffing. But when I stopped taking her phone calls, she did go out to the house.'

'Your house?' His mother was appalled. And, when Jack nodded, she asked, 'She spoke to Rachel?'

'Yeah. She told her I wanted a divorce because we were having a baby.'

'Holy Mother of God!' Maggie crossed herself before she spoke again. 'So Rachel knows about her? About what she's saying?'

'Yes, she knows.' Jack's tone was flat.

'But she didn't believe her?'

'I'm not sure what Rachel believes,' admitted Jack honestly, knowing he could never tell his mother how she'd reacted that night.

'But she came here. Surely that proves she believes you?'

'I thought so,' Jack conceded. 'Now I'm not so sure.'

'But this woman must be mad!'

'Close.'

Maggie shook her head. 'It's incredible.' Then she frowned. 'I wonder why she chose you? Karen, I mean. Did she know you and Rachel were having problems?'

'Maybe.' Jack wished he didn't have to talk about it. It was too depressing. 'I'm sure she knew about Rachel losing the babies. After I'd told everyone I was going to be a father, I don't see how she could have avoided it. God, if only I'd never invited her out. I must have been mad!'

'Hmm.' His mother was considering what he'd said.

'I'm beginning to see a pattern here. There's no woman more vulnerable to emotional blackmail than a woman who's lost a baby. For Karen to claim she was having *your* child was a clever idea.'

'Whatever.' Jack felt exhausted suddenly. He grimaced. 'It's good to know you don't think she could have fancied me.'

'Well, of course she did,' exclaimed his mother impatiently. 'That goes without saying. Aren't you the image of your father, and himself still a fine-looking man even after all these years?' She paused for a moment. 'Whose idea was it that you should take her out?'

Jack scowled. 'Mine, I guess.'

'Are you sure about that?'

He made a dismissive gesture. 'Like I say, she was always hanging around my suite of offices. I don't remember how I came to ask her. Maybe George suggested it. He knew I was feeling low. I don't know.'

'So come on,' his mother persisted, 'who do you think the real father of the baby might be?'

Jack was taken aback. 'How the hell would I know that?'

'But you must have thought about it?'

'Not really.' Jack was honest. 'I've been too busy trying to extricate myself from Karen's lies to worry about who else might be involved.'

'Then you should have.' Maggie tutted. 'For heaven's sake, Jack, it could be someone you know.'

Jack was skeptical. 'It could be anyone.'

'I don't think so. Haven't you heard the expression about the world being a small place? In my opinion, scandal usually sticks close to home.'

'Yeah, right.' Jack saw no point in hashing over the

possible suspects now. Whoever it was, they were unlikely to own up.

'Could it be someone from the office?' His mother was like a dog with a bone she wouldn't let go.

Jack heaved a sigh. 'Like I say, it could be anyone, Ma. Fox Construction employs over a hundred people in the Plymouth office.'

'And you say Karen used to work in George Thomas's office. Is there anyone there she might have been involved with?'

'Ma!'

'What about George? He's not much older than you, is he?'

'George!' Jack was incredulous. 'Ma, George is married with three teenage daughters. In all the time I've known him I've never known him look at another woman.'

His mother shrugged. 'Well, Karen is persistent, you'll have to give her that. And she's one of those women who attracts a certain type of man.'

'Give it up, Ma.'

'You know the sort I mean. Men who like women to have plenty of flesh on their bones. Overweight redheads with big breasts.'

Jack couldn't prevent a rueful smile from touching his lips. 'You really liked her, didn't you?' he said sardonically.

'No. I didn't like her at all,' declared Maggie Riordan fiercely. 'She's got gold-digger written all over her. If you ask me, she expects you to buy her off. She knows you can't prove a thing until she has that baby.'

Jack stared at her. 'Are you saying that you think I *should* pay her off?'

'No, I'm not.' His mother sounded cross. 'But I do think you should give some thought to that other matter. If George Thomas isn't involved, who is?'

Rachel spent the next week working on the drawings for the current *Benjie* book. She was behind schedule, and even now it was difficult to concentrate with so much on her mind.

Going to Ireland hadn't been planned, but she was so glad she had. She just wished she hadn't had to come home alone. That had definitely not been part of her plan.

She probably wouldn't have made the trip at all if George Thomas hadn't suggested it. When she'd had no word from Jack, she'd phoned the acting managing director and asked him if he knew when her husband intended to come back. He'd been a little vague, and she'd had the impressions that Jack hadn't confided in him either. But he had maintained that, in his opinion, Jack was depressed as well as burned out physically. He was sure Jack would be pleased to see her. And in the event he'd been right.

But now she was back in England again all Rachel's old fears were surfacing. Okay, she accepted that Jack was rundown, but he hadn't seemed depressed to her. Was it just seeing her again that had lifted his spirits? Or was he really feeling much better? And, if so, why hadn't he come home with her?

Someone tapped at the studio door and Rachel turned eagerly, half hoping her thoughts had conjured him up. But it was Mrs Grady who had interrupted her, a look of apology on her weathered face.

'I'm just letting you know I'm off to the village, Mrs Riordan,' she said diffidently. 'I'm going to the Post Office, but I shouldn't be long. Is there anything I can get you?'

Just a husband, thought Rachel gloomily, but she managed a smile for the housekeeper. 'I'm fine, Mrs Grady. I'm hoping to get this chapter finished in about an hour. Then I'm going to have a nice relaxing soak in the bath.'

'Good for you.' The housekeeper smiled in return. 'So—I'll see you later.'

'I hope so.'

The housekeeper nodded and headed back towards the house. Rachel heaved a sigh, but returned to her easel. She had quite a bit of work to do before she could take the promised break.

It must have been about ten minutes after Mrs Grady's departure that Rachel again got the feeling she was no longer alone. It wasn't a pleasant feeling this time, and she hoped Mrs Grady had locked the gates behind her. She was probably paranoid, she knew, but since Karen's unwelcome invasion, and Jack's departure for Ireland, Rachel had become intensely security conscious.

The feeling wouldn't go away, and after mixing the wrong colours and spilling water over one of her finished drawings Rachel threw her paintbrush down in disgust. To hell with it, she thought. She'd finish the chapter tomorrow. Jack wasn't the only one who was feeling stressed.

But she had respect for the tools of her trade and, picking the paintbrush up again, she washed it and the others before closing up the studio. The ruined drawing couldn't be rescued, but it would dry out overnight. She'd feel more positive in the morning, after she'd had a good night's sleep.

She was locking the door of the studio when she saw Karen Johnson. The other woman was resting on the low wall that edged the patio area, and although it was a fairly cool August day, Karen's face was flushed bright red. She stood when Rachel turned towards her, and although she wanted to ignore it, Rachel couldn't fail to see her bulging stomach tugging her summer dress out of shape.

'Hello, Rachel,' she said a little breathily. 'Long time, no see.'

'Not long enough,' retorted Rachel, dropping the keys to the studio in the pocket of her jeans. 'How did you get in?'

'Why? Because you've got this place locked up like Fort Knox?' Karen snorted. 'You forget, I've been here before. I noticed the house backed onto the cove. I took a chance that there might be a way to get up to the house from the beach. And I was right.'

Rachel stared at her. 'You've come up from Foliot Cove?' No wonder Karen was red-faced. In her condition it must have been quite a climb.

'I had to.' Karen fanned herself with an unsteady hand. 'I saw your housekeeper go out, but the gates closed behind her and I knew I couldn't climb over the wall. So, as I say, I drove back to the village.' She gave a smirk. 'Not so secure, are you?'

Silently, Rachel admitted that she was right. If Karen could climb the steps from the cove, so could anyone else. A thief, for instance—though there was little crime in Market Abbas.

'Anyway, you've wasted your time,' she said now. 'I've got no intention of speaking to you. And if you're looking for Jack, he's not here.'

'I know that.' Karen spoke disparagingly. 'For heaven's sake, haven't I just spent the last few weeks with him in Ballyryan?' She shook her head, as if amused by Rachel's expression. 'You don't believe me, do you?' She fumbled in her bag and brought out a cardboard folder. 'Here, look at that. It's the ticket to Dublin I bought just over a week ago. The day you arrived and ruined everything.'

CHAPTER ELEVEN

'I DON'T BELIEVE you.'

Rachel's words were clear and convincing, but deep inside she wondered if she really meant them. For pity's sake, Karen must know that in a matter of months her lies—if they were lies—would be exposed. There were tests they could do to ascertain if Jack really was the baby's father. Why was she persisting with this when there was no future in it?

'Look at the ticket! Look at it!'

Karen was waving the folder in front of her face, and because the woman was getting agitated Rachel complied. Sure enough, the ticket was a single from Wexford to Dublin—the same train she'd used in the opposite direction—and dated the same day she'd arrived in Ballyryan. But what did it actually prove?

Only that Karen had been there.

Rachel's stomach clenched. Why did Karen have a ticket to Dublin? A used ticket at that. How long had she stayed in Ballyryan, and what had she been doing there? Was the reason it was a single ticket because she'd travelled out with Jack in the Aston Martin?

Oh, God! Rachel felt sick. Karen must have seen Jack.

She *must* have. And, once again, he hadn't mentioned it to her. What secrets was he keeping from her? Was this the real reason why he hadn't come home?

The unwilling memory of him standing outside the cottage when she'd arrived came back to her. He'd looked ill, she remembered. Pale and sweating—and guilty as hell? Why hadn't she suspected something then? Why had she let him spirit her away for the rest of the morning? He might have seen her coming and left his parents to get Karen out of the house before they got back.

No!

Rachel stifled the agonised cry that was rising inside her. She couldn't believe that the man who'd seemed so delighted to see her, who'd taken her to that enchanted place and made such sweet, passionate love to her, was living a secret life. It wasn't true. Jack had had nothing on his conscience, she would swear it. And, once again, she was letting Karen call the shots.

'This means nothing,' she said now, dropping the offending ticket folder onto the teak-topped patio table. 'You're wasting your time, Karen. I love Jack and he loves me.'

'You think?' Karen was contemptuous. 'I wonder what I have to do to make you believe me? Describe the inside of his parents' home, perhaps?' She put a taunting finger to her lips. 'Let me see: oh, yes, there's a narrow hall that runs from the front of the cottage through to the kitchen. The parlour's whitewashed, with lots of little tables covered in knick-knacks. Maggie likes things like that, and she's got some very pretty ceramic mugs. I liked her a lot, and Jack's father looks exactly like him, doesn't he? They both made me feel really welcome.'

'I don't believe you.' Somehow Rachel found the courage to answer her. 'Do you honestly think being able to describe the cottage proves anything?' She managed a short laugh. 'Honestly, Karen, a salesperson could learn as much.'

Karen's face, already red, darkened alarmingly. 'You can't do this,' she said desperately. 'You can't blind yourself to what's going on.'

'Nothing's going on,' said Rachel, hoping against hope that she was right. 'Now, I want you to leave. I'll even open the gates for you. I wouldn't want you to fall down the cliff.'

Karen moved her head from side to side. Then, with a lightning change of tactics, she sank down onto one of the patio chairs. 'I feel sick,' she said. 'I'm dehydrated after climbing all those steps. Please, I need a drink. Even *you* couldn't deny me a glass of water.'

Rachel shook her head. But it was obvious that Karen was extremely hot. Maybe she was dehydrated. Maybe a woman in her condition perspired more freely. There were certainly areas of darkness beneath her arms and between her breasts.

'All right,' she said, giving in. 'Wait here. I'll get you a glass of water.'

She used her keys to open the French doors into the garden room. She had no intention of opening the doors into the drawing room and risking Karen taking up residence in there again. Then, evading the urns of plants that were spilling blossom and greenery onto the terracotta tiles, she left the room by the hall door and hurried down the corridor to the kitchen.

She couldn't have been more than two minutes, but when she got back there was no one on the patio. Frowning, she looked all about her, but there was no sign of Karen anywhere. Had she gone? Rachel couldn't believe she'd been that lucky. But the only way she could have left was by the cliff steps, and, putting the glass of water down on the table, she went through the gate that led out onto the cliff.

Like the patio, the cliff steps were deserted. Surely Karen hadn't had time to reach the beach? But, apart from a man walking his dog, the beach was empty, too. It was if the woman had disappeared into thin air.

The first intimation she had that someone was behind her was a rush of air across the back of her bare arms and the sound of laboured breathing in her ear. Then a hand hit her firmly in the small of her back, knocking her instantly off balance, and before she could recover a second punch sent her over the edge.

She fell, terror causing her to cartwheel her arms and legs in an effort to save herself. Shrubs and gorse bushes punctuated her descent, but although she grabbed at them they weren't strong enough to hold her. All she got for her pains were scratched and bleeding palms and a sickening blow to her forehead.

Deliverance came from a totally unexpected source. Rachel had virtually given up hope of saving herself, but her mind refused to countenance the image of her body sprawled on the sand below. Grabbing for the stunted root of a tree growing from a crack in the cliff-face was just an automatic reflex. Her hands felt numb; her brain was closing down, she was preparing herself to die.

The sudden savage cinching about her waist drove all the breath out of her. But it also kicked her brain into action again. By some miracle, her flight into oblivion had been halted. How, she didn't yet know. She hadn't crashed onto the ground. With tears almost blinding her, she realised she was hanging free, some thirty feet above the beach.

Gasping for breath, she tried to understand what had happened. It felt as if someone had lassoed her, but she knew that wasn't the answer. Yet something was digging into her waist, preventing her from falling. She tried to look down, to see what it was, but she didn't dare move too much in case she started to fall again.

Then she heard a shout.

Panic gripped her. Now that her mind was working again, the thought that it might be Karen, climbing down the steps to finish what she'd started, brought a cry of terror to her throat.

But it was a man's voice, she realised. A man who advised her not to move an inch until he reached her. He was climbing up from below, and she guessed with relief that he must be the man she'd seen walking his dog on the beach.

'Well, I think you're mad!'

Maggie Riordan came into the bedroom where her son was packing a canvas duffel bag and regarded him with dark accusing eyes.

'I know.'

With a rueful glance in his mother's direction, Jack continued what he was doing, hoping she'd realise that, whatever either of his parents said, he had to go back. He'd already booked the car onto the next morning's ferry, and he intended to get up early and drive to Rosslare. He hadn't heard a word from Rachel since she'd left two weeks ago, all calls to her mobile had been transferred immediately to voicemail, and he was worried.

He'd considered calling Mrs Grady, but pride—and a

certain amount of reluctance to involve the housekeeper—
had deterred him from doing so. For all he knew, Rachel
might not have told Mrs Grady what had happened when
she came to Ireland, and it would have been embarrassing
having to explain to the housekeeper that the estrangement
that had existed between them for so long was no longer
a reality.

Or was it? Wasn't that the real reason he'd decided to
pack up and go home? Because he couldn't believe they
had heard the last of Karen?

His father appeared behind his mother then, laying a
soothing hand on her shoulder. 'Leave him, Maggie,' he
said quietly. 'Jack knows his own business better than we
do.'

'But he's only been here for five weeks,' protested his
wife frustratedly. 'You know yourself his doctor advised
him to take at least six months away from work.'

'Do you mind not talking as if I wasn't in the room?'
Jack exclaimed tersely. 'And I haven't said I'm going back
to work, have I? As a matter of fact, I've been considering
making some changes when I get back. Not the least of
them being delegating some of my work so Rachel and I
can spend more time together.'

'Well, that's the most sensible thing you've said, so it
is,' declared his mother, nodding, and without another
word she came into the room and slapped away his hand
as he attempted to put a rolled tee shirt into his bag. 'Let
me do that,' she added, taking the tee shirt from his hand
and folding it to her satisfaction. 'Men! They haven't the
first idea how to pack clothes.'

Jude Riordan exchanged a smile with his son. Then,
propping his shoulder against the frame of the door, he
said, 'Have you ever thought of buying yourselves a sec-

ond home here in the village? Ryan House has been empty these three years past, and although I've no doubt it needs a canny thing doing to it, sure you've got the money to make it habitable.'

Jack stared at his farther. 'Ryan House!' He frowned. 'But that place is derelict.'

'It is now,' agreed his father. 'But isn't that the kind of work you could do? Sure, I know you're an architect, Jack, and you're not used to getting your hands dirty, but I can't think of a better project to keep you from being bored.'

Jack was about to say that in any case Ryan House was too big for his and Rachel's needs, but he didn't. Maybe it *was* too big, but the idea of renovating the old place did appeal to him. 'How much do they want for it?' he asked, guessing his father had done his homework before speaking. And after Jude had delivered his answer he was pleasantly surprised.

'Maybe you've got something there, Dad,' he said, aware that his mother was listening. 'I'll certainly think about it. I'd have to discuss it with Rachel first, of course, but it's an interesting idea.'

And it was something to keep his mind occupied the next morning, as he drove to the busy ferry terminal that served Wexford and the surrounding area. He didn't know what Rachel would think of it, but it was true that she could work almost anywhere.

Apart from a certain amount of apprehension, he was feeling okay, he thought. The weeks spent at Ballyryan hadn't completely banished the occasional pounding in his chest, or the fluttering heartbeat that could make him feel so sickeningly light-headed. But he hadn't experienced any dizziness since the morning both Rachel and Karen had turned up, and the rest had definitely done him good.

He felt—what? Almost seventy per cent—which was a good result, considering he'd only had a few weeks away from the rat race, instead of the six months the doctor had recommended.

The ferry crossing to Fishguard was both fast and efficient, and pretty soon he was on the M4 heading for the junction with the M5 and home. He called Rachel again when he stopped for a mid-afternoon bottle of water at a service area. But once again there was no reply, and he had to exert a massive amount of self-control not to let her continuing silence faze him. He'd see her soon, he told himself. And it was probably better to have their first conversation face to face.

It was after he'd passed Exeter and was driving along the A38 towards the turn-off to Market Abbas that he had his first intimation that he wasn't as fit as he'd thought he was. He was finding it increasingly difficult to keep his eyes open, exhaustion pulling at him in bone-deep waves of fatigue. It occurred to him that he'd been a fool to attempt to drive so far when he wasn't used to it. Besides, he'd made the original journey in two stages, staying overnight in Swansea. He should have thought about that when he'd decided to come home.

It was early evening when he reached Market Abbas. The village, which was chiefly one main street with several arteries leading to it, was almost deserted. The few shops were closed, of course, though the three pubs appeared to be doing good business. Years ago he and Rachel had used to walk down to the village on summer evenings and enjoy a drink on the terrace of the Ship Inn, which overlooked the ocean.

Now Jack drove doggedly on, desperate to reach his destination. He was feeling distinctly light-headed, probably because he was so weary, and he couldn't wait to get out of the car.

The gates to the house he shared with Rachel were closed, however, and he realised he should have had the sense to call ahead. As it was, he would have to get out and identify himself via the intercom. The only other keys on his key ring were those that opened the house.

Mrs Grady answered when he pressed the button. 'Why, Mr Riordan!' she exclaimed, and he could have sworn there was a note of nervous anxiety in her voice. Or was his brain playing tricks with him? 'What are you doing here?'

Jack endeavoured to control his impatience. 'I live here, Mrs Grady,' he said curtly. 'Look, will you just stop messing around and open the gates? I'm tired. I don't have time for this. I need to lie down.'

'Oh—well—I suppose—in the circumstances...'

Mrs Grady was definitely on edge, and Jack didn't know why. What had Rachel said to her, for God's sake? This was hardly the welcome home he'd expected.

Then, when he was on the point of losing his temper, he saw the gates shudder before beginning to swing inward. With a relieved sigh, he walked heavily back to the car. Where the hell was Rachel anyway? he wondered. He should have called ahead. He would have if he'd suspected she might not be here.

He parked the car to one side of the front doors and hauled his duffel bag out of the boot. By that time Mrs Grady was standing on the front steps. She looked much the same as usual, but she was wringing her hands, which usually meant she was worried about something.

'Can I help you with that?' she asked, as Jack slung the strap of the duffel bag over his shoulder and almost overbalanced from its weight. 'Oh, dear.' She gazed at him with

obvious concern. 'You do look tired, don't you? Here—
let me take your arm.'

'I can manage.' In spite of his exhaustion, Jack drew the
line at leaning on a woman. He locked the car and started
up the three shallow steps that widened into a porch. Tubs
of impatiens and geraniums made vivid splashes of colour
against the mellow brickwork, but Jack hardly noticed as
he entered the house.

Then, glancing back at the housekeeper, who was following him, he said flatly, 'Where's my wife?'

It was just as well he'd carried on across the entrance
hall into the drawing room. He heard Mrs Grady take a
deep breath, and then she said quietly, 'She's not here, Mr
Riordan.'

'Not here?' Slinging his bag onto the floor, Jack sank
down onto the arm of one of the sofas. Then, as a heavy
weight descended on his shoulders, he added, 'Where is
she?'

'I—er—she's staying with Ms Robards, Mr Riordan.'
Mrs Grady had paused in the doorway, and she allowed a
moment for her astonishing words to sink in. 'After—after
the—er—accident—'

'What accident?' Despite his own weariness, Jack's reaction was one of shock. 'I didn't know Lucy had had an
accident, dammit. Why didn't Rachel let me know?'

'Because it wasn't Ms Robards who had the accident,'
said Mrs Grady unhappily. 'It was your wife.'

'Rachel!' Jack was horrified now. But he was glad he'd
taken the opportunity to sit down. 'My God, why didn't
somebody tell me?'

'I wanted to.' Mrs Grady spoke urgently, and, even
though Jack was tempted to ask her why the hell she hadn't

in that case, he was inclined to believe her. 'But—well, people said—'

'People? What people?' Jack tried not to get angry with her. 'What are you talking about?'

'Um—well, Mr Thomas said we shouldn't worry you unnecessarily—'

'George should mind his own bloody business!'

'And Ms Robards—'

Jack growled. 'That figures,' he muttered darkly. 'So what happened? Was it a car accident?'

'No.' Mrs Grady looked uncomfortable now. Then, shaking her head, she went on, 'I don't think it's my place to tell you what happened, Mr Riordan. All I can say is, it's lucky Mrs Riordan wasn't badly injured.'

Jack's shoulders sagged and he raked a hand over his damp forehead. Although he felt infinitely worse now than he'd done before, he had to know what was going on. He thought about getting to his feet and baulked at the effort. 'I've got to see her.'

Mrs Grady watched him with troubled eyes. 'Oh, Mr Riordan, I don't think—'

'What?' Jack wasn't in the mood to be tactful. 'What don't you think? That I should go and see my own wife? She's had an accident, dammit. An accident you refuse to tell me about. And for some reason she's staying with a woman who hates my guts. What do you expect me to do? Wait until the morning and give her a call?'

'That might be the wisest course,' murmured Mrs Grady unhappily. 'I know you're worried—'

'Damn right!'

'—but Mrs Riordan's just getting over the accident. And after what that woman said she might not want to—'

'What woman?' demanded Jack harshly. But he knew. 'My God, are you telling me that Karen Johnson's been here again?' He gathered his strength and pushed himself to his feet. 'When? When was she here? Is that why you don't think Rachel will want to see me?'

Mrs Grady chewed on her lower lip. 'I—I thought you knew.'

'Knew what?'

'About Miss Johnson's visit.'

'Well, I didn't.' Jack swayed back on his heels. 'Look, why don't you stop clucking like an old hen and tell me what this is all about? Are you saying Rachel's accident had something to do with Karen?' He winced at the sudden tightness in his chest. 'Dammit, woman, did she run her down?'

'It was nothing like that.' Mrs Grady had evidently noticed his agitation and she attempted to reassure him. 'Actually, Miss Johnson had nothing to do with the accident. It happened after she'd gone. I know Mrs Riordan was upset, so she might have been indirectly involved, but—'

'For God's sake!' Jack clenched his fists. 'Will you stop waffling around. What happened? Tell me!'

Mrs Grady shifted uneasily. 'I don't know exactly what happened. I'd gone into the village, you see. But—well, it seems Mrs Riordan had gone for a walk on the cliffs, and—and she fell.'

Jack blanched. 'Over the cliff?'

'Apparently.' Mrs Grady's hands were twisting together again. 'According to the man who managed to rescue her, it was the belt loop on her jeans that saved her life. It—it caught on a root or something. Without it—'

Her voice trailed away and Jack sank numbly back onto the sofa. He could imagine only too well what would have happened without that lifeline. And, however innocent it seemed, he was fairly sure Karen must have said something to cause Rachel so much distress that she'd been careless. She'd walked on those cliffs a hundred times before.

'Anyway, as I say, Mrs Riordan's all right now,' the housekeeper continued, evidently deciding there was no point in holding anything back. 'She was lucky Mr Harris was walking his dog on the beach and saw what happened. He had the presence of mind to call the emergency services and—'

'I get the picture.' Jack was sweating now, but somehow he managed to get to his feet again. He'd been right to be suspicious of what Karen might do, he thought unsteadily. But why had Rachel taken it into her head to go and stay with Lucy Robards when it would have been so much more convenient for Lucy to come here?

'Anyway, I don't think you should go out again this evening,' Mrs Grady ventured, braving the bitter look he cast in her direction. 'Forgive me for being frank, Mr Riordan, but you don't look at all well. Why don't you rest for a while and let me make you something light for supper? You can go and see Mrs Riordan in the morning.'

'You're kidding, right?' Jack stared at her disbelievingly. 'You don't seriously expect me to do that? My God, I have to see Rachel. I have to see for myself that she's all right.'

'Well, I don't think you should take too much for granted, Mr Riordan.'

Jack had started towards her, but now he halted, nonplussed. 'What?'

Mrs Grady sighed. 'Well, Mrs Riordan was very upset about what Miss Johnson said to her. I don't think she believed it all, but when she was in the hospital—'

'She was in *hospital?*'

'Just overnight,' said Mrs Grady hurriedly. 'And she was a bit—hysterical, perhaps. But, anyway, I believe she told Ms Robards that Miss Johnson had insisted she'd been staying with you in Ireland.'

'What?'

'Miss Johnson even had a ticket, Mr Riordan. One she said she'd used the morning Mrs Riordan arrived in Ballyryan herself.'

'Dear God!'

'But if you say Miss Johnson wasn't there, that she was making the whole thing up, I'm sure Mrs Riordan will believe you.'

CHAPTER TWELVE

'DO YOU THINK I ought to go and see him?'

Rachel was standing in the bay window of her friend's living room, staring out at the rain. She was purposely keeping her back to Lucy so she couldn't see her expression. But she was afraid the desperation she was feeling must be evident in her voice.

It was four weeks since the accident that had almost killed her. It had been an accident, she assured herself. She refused to believe it had been anything else. And in all that time, she had had no word from her husband, even though she knew he had returned to Market Abbas over two weeks ago.

Lucy Robards, who was lounging in an armchair, enjoying the mug of coffee Rachel had just made, heaved a sigh. 'Are you mad?' she demanded incredulously. 'Jack knows where you are. He's known where you are for weeks—ever since you had that fall, for heaven's sake. Why would you want to go and see him? To ask him if he still loves you, perhaps?' She sneered. 'I think we know the answer to that, don't we?'

'Do we?

Rachel's response drew another impatient exclamation from her friend, but she ignored it. Lucy didn't understand. She didn't understand anything. Rachel didn't understand a lot herself, but she still couldn't believe that everything Karen had said was true.

She shivered. In spite of her determination to regard what had happened as an aberration on her part, she still trembled at the thought of the other woman's name. But no one had pushed her off the cliff, she assured herself. She had imagined the hand in the small of her back, the blow that had sent her careening into space.

Nevertheless, the nightmares—in which Karen did indeed play a part in what had happened—continued to torment her, and she'd wake in a lather of fear and apprehension. On those occasions it would take hours before she could get back to sleep.

A feeling of sickness welled in her throat and she fought to control it. She must not let Lucy suspect that anything Karen had said or done had forced her out of her own home, even if it was true. No, she was staying here because she hadn't wanted to return to the scene of the accident. Not yet, anyway. But if Jack was there…

'You're not seriously considering going back to him?' Lucy got up now and came to stand beside her, forcing Rachel to look her way. Then she caught her breath. 'My God, you *are* considering it, aren't you?' She shook her head. 'And you're crying! Oh, Rachel, what am I going to do with you?'

Rachel shook her head, hurriedly smudging the tears from her cheeks with a clumsy hand. 'I just find it hard to believe that Jack would come back to Market Abbas without coming to see me if he knew where I was,' she mumbled. 'Whatever his faults, Jack's not like that.'

'That was before Karen Johnson got her claws into him,' retorted Lucy shortly. 'And don't you think Mrs

Grady will have told him where you're staying? Haven't you ever considered that the reason you haven't seen him is because he's ashamed?'

Rachel sniffed. 'Yes.'

'There you are, then.'

'But what did he say?' Rachel persisted suddenly. 'When George phoned and told him I'd had a—a fall, how did he react?'

'You'd have to ask George that,' declared Lucy, losing patience. 'Honestly, Rachel, what more do you need to convince you that Jack's been lying to you? A signed confession?'

Rachel pressed her lips together, feeling the panicked nausea rising inside her once more. She couldn't believe that in a matter of weeks her life had fallen apart so completely. When had Karen first come to see her? The middle of June? It was the beginning of September now, and if it didn't sound so pathetic she would say she was a broken woman.

To her relief, the phone rang at that moment, and although she knew a moment's hope, Lucy's response revealed that it was only her friend's London agent. But at least it gave Rachel an excuse to leave, and, going up to her room, she closed the door and sat down on the bed.

What was she going to do? she fretted. She couldn't go on living with Lucy, however willing the other woman might be. For one thing, she'd done no work since the accident, and although her publisher had been remarkably understanding, sooner or later she was going to have to finish the artwork for the book she'd started before all this happened.

She remembered the afternoon of the accident as if it were yesterday. How she'd been on edge after Mrs Grady

left, and had spilled water over one of her finished drawings. Another wave of sickness enveloped her, stronger this
time, driving her into the bathroom. She'd been right to be
on edge, she thought, as her stomach emptied itself into
the toilet. My God, whether Karen had pushed her off the
cliff or not, she'd certainly done her best to destroy the
fragile relationship burgeoning between Rachel and her
husband.

Back in the bedroom again, she surveyed herself in the
dressing table mirror. Heavens, what a ghoul, she thought,
scrubbing her pale cheeks with her fingers to try and bring
some colour into them. Her hair looked lank and listless,
and she was losing weight. Hardly the image to present to
the man you believed was cheating on you.

Or did she believe that? Crazy as it seemed, bearing in
mind the facts of the case, she couldn't totally rid her mind
of the thought that if Karen had been so sure of Jack's in-
tentions she wouldn't have felt the need to come and torment her. Or would she? Perhaps she was afraid that if
Rachel divorced her husband she would ruin him financially. How much easier it would be if Rachel was dead,
allowing Jack total control of both the finances and the
company.

That thought caused another wave of nausea, and
Rachel was emerging from the bathroom a second time
when Lucy knocked at her door and called, 'Can I come
in?'

Rachel would have preferred to say no, but it was
Lucy's house, after all, so she answered, 'Of course.'

Lucy opened the door and put her head into the room.
'You okay?' she asked, with some concern, and although
Rachel felt anything but, she nodded.

'I was going to have a lie-down, that's all,' she said, not

altogether truthfully, putting a deliberately upbeat note in her voice. 'What did Stephen want?'

'Well, that's what I wanted to tell you,' said Lucy ruefully. 'He wants me to go up to London again. He's arranged a meeting with someone who's interested in expanding the column into his chain of store magazines. I can't tell you who it is until the deal's actually signed, but take my word for it—this is a big opportunity for me.'

'That's wonderful!' Rachel was sincerely pleased for her friend. 'Will it mean more money?'

'You better believe it.' Lucy chuckled. 'At least another ten thou a year at the minimum.'

'How exciting!'

'Do you mean that?'

'What do you mean, do I mean it?' Rachel was slightly offended. 'Why wouldn't I mean it?'

'Oh…' Lucy was clearly uncomfortable. 'The fact that my career seems to be taking off just when you—well, when you're not able to work.'

'You think?' Rachel wondered if that was strictly true. Maybe she'd feel better if she *was* working. It might help her to get her confidence back, she thought. 'Well, I'm delighted,' she insisted. Then, a little apprehensively, 'When are you leaving?'

'Well, that's the thing.' Lucy bit her lip. 'Would you mind if I went up to town this afternoon? The meeting's at lunchtime tomorrow, but I'd prefer to stay overnight and give myself a little time to prepare.' She paused. 'You can come, too, if you feel up to it.'

'Oh, no.' Rachel dropped down onto the side of the bed again, refusing to admit to the panic she was feeling at the thought of being on her own again for the first time since the accident. 'I'd just be in the way.' She paused. 'I'll be all right here. I might even buy myself a pad and start making some sketches for when I can get back to work. Don't you worry. I'll be fine.'

'If you're sure?'

It was obvious Lucy was relieved, and Rachel managed a weak smile. 'Good luck,' she said. 'You deserve it.'

However, that afternoon, after the taxi had left, taking Lucy to Plymouth to catch the London train, the cottage did feel unpleasantly empty. Lucy did have a cleaning woman, but she only came in twice a week for a couple of hours, and Lucy had little to do with her neighbours.

In consequence, Rachel felt horribly alone. And isolated. Not that Karen knew where she was, of course, and even if she did what could she do about it? What could she want to do about it?

Murder her, perhaps?

But that was stupid and absurd. She had no proof that Karen had intended to do anything except drive a verbal wedge between her and Jack for a second time. Even the man who'd called the emergency services thought Rachel had slipped and fallen on the damp grass. And, because it had sounded ridiculous to claim that someone had pushed her, Rachel hadn't contradicted him.

Indeed, over the weeks since it had happened she'd succeeded in convincing her conscious mind, at least, that she had imagined it. It was only now, with Lucy on her way to London and the certain knowledge that she would be spending that night and all the next day on her own, that those suspicions were stirring again.

When the doorbell rang in the late afternoon, Rachel almost jumped out of her skin. She'd turned on the television in the hope that the quiz show taking place on the screen would provide her with some much-needed company. But the knowledge that there was someone outside now, waiting for admittance, showed the virtual images up for what they really were: a useless substitute.

She didn't have to answer it, she told herself. She wished now she'd chosen to watch television in the kitchen, which wasn't visible from the front of the house. As it was, if the visitor happened to glance through the window they'd see her. Edging across the room, she insinuated herself against the wall and squinted through a break in the curtains.

Then she almost collapsed with relief. It was MrsGrady. She hadn't seen the housekeeper for ages—not since the week after the accident, actually. Until now, she hadn't thought anything about it, but it suddenly occurred to her that Mrs Grady must be looking after Jack. Was that why she'd stayed away?

It certainly put a different slant on the reason for her visit. If she'd come to plead Jack's case, Rachel didn't know if she should let her in. After all, this was Lucy's house, not hers, and there was no question that her friend would not approve.

The bell rang again, and, realising she couldn't just ignore it, Rachel took a deep breath and stepped out into the hall. Then, plastering a polite smile in place, she walked to the door and pulled it open.

'Mrs Grady,' she said, and even to her own ears her voice sounded stilted. 'This is a surprise.'

'I was beginning to think you were out,' Mrs Grady responded, with a corresponding lack of conviction. 'How are you, Mrs Riordan? I've been thinking about you. A lot.'

'Have you?' Rachel lifted her shoulders in a dismissing gesture. 'Well, as you can see, I'm feeling much better.'

'Are you?' Mrs Grady glanced over her shoulder. 'Is Ms Robards here?'

'I—no.' Rachel couldn't lie to her own housekeeper. 'She's just left for London, actually. She has an important meeting with her agent.'

'Good.' Mrs Grady nodded. Then, in a low, urgent voice, 'May I come in?'

Rachel was taken aback. She had thought the woman was just making a courtesy call, and it was disconcerting to be put on the spot. 'Um—well, I am rather busy.'

'Watching television?' Mrs Grady proved she was more astute than Rachel had given her credit for. 'Look, Mrs Riordan, I realise you think you have your own reasons for not inviting me in, but believe me you'll be sorry if you don't.'

Rachel swallowed. 'I beg your pardon—'

'Oh, now, that sounded melodramatic, didn't it?' Mrs Grady shifted a little awkwardly. 'I'm sorry. But honestly, Mrs Riordan, there are—there are things you need to know.'

Rachel stiffened. 'If this is about Karen Johnson—'

'It's not. Well, perhaps indirectly.'

'Mrs Grady—'

'Please.' The housekeeper gazed at her beseechingly. 'This is important, and I don't have a lot of time. If Mr Riordan knew where I was—'

'You mean he doesn't?'

'Of course not.' Mrs Grady glanced up and down the street as if to assure herself she hadn't been followed. 'He's—well, he's sleeping at the moment. But—'

Rachel blinked. 'Sleeping?' she echoed incredulously. 'But it's—' she glanced at her watch '—it's nearly five o'clock.'

Mrs Grady's face took on an expression of resignation. 'I know,' she said flatly. 'Like I say, I need to talk to you.'

Rachel stood aside without a word and the housekeeper stepped into the narrow hall. 'It's the first door on the right,' said Rachel absently, and then closing the door, hastened after her.

Mrs Grady was standing in the middle of the room, evidently unsure of herself, and Rachel gestured towards one of the armchairs that flanked the empty fireplace. 'Sit down.' She perched on the chair opposite, elbows propped on her thighs. 'What is this all about? Is Jack ill again?'

Mrs Grady sighed. 'He's—not well,' she conceded reluctantly. 'As a matter of fact, he hasn't been well for a while.'

'I know that.' Rachel was impatient. 'He told me he'd been working too hard. That was why he went to Ireland. Because he needed a break.'

'Yes.' Mrs Grady bit her lip. 'That is what he told you. I know that.' She paused. 'But did you never think that taking six months away from the office was rather excessive for someone who'd just been overworking?'

'Six months?' Rachel shook her head. 'He told me he was going to Ireland for a month—six weeks at the outside. He didn't say anything about six months!'

'No, well—I don't suppose he wanted to worry you.'

'Worry me?' Rachel got to her feet now, pushing her hands deep into the pockets of her shorts. 'He didn't worry me, no. But you are, Mrs Grady. What are you trying to say? That Jack lied about his condition?'

Mrs Grady looked discomforted. 'He didn't—lie, exactly.'

'But he didn't tell the whole truth, right?' Rachel could feel the panic rising inside her, but she had to keep control of her emotions. 'Yes, he's very good at that,' she added bitterly.

'You don't understand, Mrs Riordan.'

'What don't I understand? That Jack didn't want to tell me he'd been advised to take six months off instead of six weeks? Why was that, I wonder? Were the demands of leading a double life getting too much for him?'

'Mr Riordan hasn't been leading a double life.' Mrs Grady rose from her chair with unexpected dignity. 'I can't believe you still think he has. But, if you do, I don't think there's any point in my continuing with this.' She looped the strap of her handbag over her arm and started for the door. 'It's time I was getting back anyway.'

'No. Wait!' Rachel couldn't let her go without explaining her situation. 'I'm sorry. I know I sound bitter, but it has been a pretty traumatic time for me, too.'

Mrs Grady nodded. 'The accident? Yes, I can understand that.'

'And—and the things that woman said.' Rachel pressed her hands together. 'If—if they weren't true, don't you think Jack should have told me?'

Mrs Grady hesitated. 'The accident was four weeks ago, Mrs Riordan, but you're still staying with Ms Robards, aren't you?'

'And you know why.'

'Do I?'

'Yes.' Rachel spread her arms now. 'I've just explained. I can't go back to the house. Not when Jack—'

'Not when Jack what?'

Rachel heaved sigh. 'Look,' she said, 'I realise you're on Jack's side—'

'I'm on nobody's side, Mrs Riordan.'

'—but even you have to admit he's been pretty cavalier

about the whole thing. Dammit, he didn't even bother to contact me when I—when I had the fall. As far as he's concerned, it never happened.'

'He didn't know,' said Mrs Grady simply, but Rachel only gave a disbelieving snort.

'Of course he knew. George Thomas phoned and told him the night I was taken to the hospital. Lucy assured me of that.'

'No.'

'What do you mean, no?'

'He didn't know,' insisted Mrs Grady doggedly. 'Like you, I thought he did. Good heavens, I'd have phoned him myself if I'd suspected that—' She broke off. 'Whatever. He definitely knew nothing about it when he first got back. I can vouch for that.'

Rachel frowned. There was something odd about that statement, but she couldn't decide what it was. Why was Mrs Grady so sure Jack was telling the truth?

Shaking her head, she let it go. 'Well, all right,' she said. 'If you're saying there was some sort of mix-up over the phone call, I'll have to accept it.' But then, on surer ground, 'Still, you can't deny he's been home for over two weeks now, and he hasn't even bothered to call or pick up the phone.'

'No.' Mrs Grady was forced to concede that, and Rachel felt a little vindication for her behaviour. But then the woman went on, 'He can't. Or won't,' she amended darkly. 'Oh, Mrs Riordan, he's going to hate me for telling you this, but—well, the night he got back from Ireland, he collapsed.'

'Collapsed!' Nausea rose in Rachel's throat again as the possibility that she might be to blame swept over her.

'And—and since he got home from the hospital,' continued Mrs Grady unhappily, 'he's been prowling round that house like a wounded beast!'

CHAPTER THIRTEEN

WHERE THE HELL was Mrs Grady?

Jack had awakened a few minutes ago, hot and thirsty, his back aching from the awkward position he'd been in while he slept. But then, when he'd flung himself into the leather chair at the bureau in the den he'd intended to riffle through his correspondence, not fall asleep.

It was the damn drugs the doctor was pumping into him that were responsible, he thought irritably, pushing himself upright, aware that his mouth tasted like the bottom of a parrot's cage. Drugs that were meant to control his heartbeat, but instead were as good as a sleeping draught in the middle of the afternoon.

His shoulders sagged. As if he needed anything to control his heartbeat now, he thought grimly. Rachel had left him, and nothing Karen Johnson did from this point on was of any interest to him. His marriage was over; his life was over. As soon as he could, he was going to resign his position at Fox Construction and take himself back to Ireland.

He pushed himself to his feet, flexed his shoulders, and ambled along to the kitchen. But Mrs Grady wasn't there. Taking down a glass, he filled it at the tap. He drank the water, staring out at the rain splashing off the roof of

Rachel's studio and wondered if she'd come back here once he was gone. Probably, he reflected dourly. It was only because he was here that she was keeping away.

Perhaps he should have phoned her. He'd wanted to. He'd been worried sick about her, goodness knew. But he doubted she'd want to hear from him. Apart from the lies Karen had told her—lies she must have believed if her continued absence was anything to go by—he hadn't wanted to admit what had happened to him when he got back. He'd been afraid he might make a fool of himself again. Dear God, collapsing in front of Mrs Grady when she'd told him about Rachel's fall hadn't been his proudest moment.

In any case, so far he'd succeeded in keeping the less palatable aspects of his condition to himself, and if he had anything to do with it it would stay that way. Rachel was a beautiful, intelligent woman, and she deserved better than a clapped-out crock who'd somehow managed to screw up every part of his life to date.

He certainly didn't believe the shrink who'd come to see him while he was in the hospital. Obviously someone who was recovering from an attack that had limited the amount of blood entering the heart might be suffering depression, but he didn't need any mind doctor telling him that there was no reason why he shouldn't make a full recovery.

His diagnosis—that Jack's problems were possibly as much psychological as physical—hadn't won him any favours. Jack refused to discuss the personal details of his marriage with anyone, least of all a stranger, even if the guy *had* found out about Rachel's miscarriages and the obvious strain that had put on both of them.

Okay, he thought now, so maybe their estrangement had played a contributory role in the way his body was behaving now. Losing three babies and the wife you loved more than life itself could do that to you. Rachel had coped with it in her own way, which hadn't made it any easier for him. Was the shrink right? In his efforts to remain in control, hadn't he allowed himself time to grieve?

Whatever, it was true that that was when he'd started spending more and more time at the office—tendering for bigger and better contracts, using work to numb his mind to other things. He'd tried to behave as if Rachel's withdrawal wasn't tearing him apart. And then, when Karen Johnson had begun stalking him...

He shuddered. Although she could do no more damage in his life, Jack couldn't prevent the twinge of desperation he felt at the harm that woman had caused. If only he hadn't felt sorry for her; if only he'd never invited her out. Then she'd have had no grounds for her accusations. She might have found someone else to use as a fall guy. The real father of her child, perhaps.

He frowned, remembering what his mother had said. Who *was* responsible for Karen's getting pregnant? Who *was* the father of the child she was carrying? Although it was hard to believe, it could be someone from the office. One of the other executives, even.

He heard the sound of Mrs Grady's car and abandoned the thought, turning to prop his hips against the unit behind him. The housekeeper must have taken the opportunity to do a bit of shopping while he was flaked out in the den. He grimaced. He knew he was a demanding patient. And she'd certainly been worth her weight in gold since she'd discovered the extent of his deception. He didn't know how he'd have managed without her these past couple of weeks.

He heard the outer door open, but although he waited expectantly Mrs Grady didn't come into the kitchen. She was probably checking up on him, he mused. He'd been dead to the world when she went out. He'd better let her know where he was before she started searching the house.

Finishing the water, he dropped the glass into the sink and pushed away from the unit. Then, opening the kitchen door, he strolled into the entrance hall.

There was no sign of the housekeeper, however. Guessing she must have gone into the den, he headed in that direction— and almost bumped into Rachel, who was just coming out.

'My God!' To his annoyance, her sudden appearance caused him to clutch at the frame of the door for support. She was the last person he'd expected to see, and he struggled to comprehend how she came to be here. 'I thought it was Mrs Grady's car I heard.'

'It was.' Rachel moistened her lips, watching him with wary eyes. 'I borrowed it.'

Jack blinked. 'So where is she?'

As if he cared where the housekeeper was, he thought grimly. Just looking at Rachel made a mockery of the plans he'd been making for his future. How could he leave, feeling as he did about her? Already his body was betraying him, responding to her nearness with an urgency that was trying to drive all sane thoughts out of his head.

She looked so good. A little thinner, perhaps, but just as beautiful as ever, in spite of her ordeal on the cliff. In a simple apricot silk vest and shorts, she brought a touch of sunshine to the rain-shadowed hallway, and if her eyes seemed a little darker than normal, it was probably because he'd startled her, too.

And then Rachel said, 'She's at Lucy's,' and suddenly everything fell into place. It wasn't a desperate need to see him again that had brought her here, but pity after what the other woman must have told her.

'I see,' he said, straightening up almost defensively. 'Mrs Grady has finally shown her true colours. All the same, I'm surprised Lucy was in favour of you coming here.'

'Lucy doesn't know,' said Rachel quickly, wishing she didn't feel so helpless. There was so much she wanted to say, but just being with Jack again was making her feel weak. In a black tee shirt and his old jeans, his feet bare below the hems of his pants, he looked lean and dark and as gorgeous as she remembered. She so much wanted to touch him, and it was hard to face his skepticism now.

Jack's lips twisted at her words. 'No kidding,' he mocked. 'Now, why didn't I think of that?'

Rachel quivered. 'Don't be like this.'

'Like what?'

'You know.' She shifted her weight from one foot to the other. 'Jack, I know you didn't know about my accident before you came home. Mrs Grady's just told me.'

'And of course Mrs Grady never lies. Only breaks confidences,' he responded, unable to keep the bitterness out of his voice. 'What else did she tell you? That I'm at death's door?' He grimaced. 'I shouldn't worry. Apparently I brought this on myself.'

'Oh, Jack, don't joke about it.'

'I'm not joking. But you have to admit it is ironic.' He shrugged. 'I dare say you think I deserve it.'

Her eyes rounded, and he could have sworn he saw tears forming in them. Suddenly he regretted what he'd said. 'Anyway, never mind that—how are you feeling now?' he asked, gazing at her intently. 'You've had a terrifying experience. Do you know how it happened?'

'Oh, I—must we talk about that?' Rachel tucked her hands beneath her arms, wishing she knew what to say. 'Um—it's you I came to see.' She hesitated. 'Are you feeling better?'

'Hey, I'm okay.' Jack spoke dismissively. 'I don't know what that old lady's told you, but the reports of my illness have been greatly exaggerated.'

'Jack—'

'No, I mean it. Like I said before I went away—I needed some time away from studying financial statements and poring over blueprints—'

'But it wasn't just tiredness, was it?' Rachel broke in. 'Mrs Grady says you have a problem with your heart.'

'Mrs Grady exaggerates.' Jack sucked in a much-needed gulp of air. 'And if you've come here to offer your sympathy, well—thanks, but it's not necessary.'

'Jack—'

'Look, I'll get over this, right? I'm not dying, or anything dramatic like that. For some reason—mostly stress, I suspect—I've developed an irregular heartbeat. Or rather I *had*. Since I've been following medical advice and taking things easy I've been feeling much better.'

Rachel gazed at him. 'Are you sure?'

'Yes, I'm sure.' Jack felt his nails digging into his palms and tried to relax. 'Sorry to disappoint you, babe, but if you've decided you want rid of me you're going to have to divorce me.'

Rachel gasped. 'I don't want rid of you.'

'No?' Jack arched a sardonic brow. 'So why are you staying at Lucy's?'

'Oh…' Once again, Rachel prevaricated. 'It's a long story.' Then, because this was so much more important than her problems, she hurried on, 'Have you any idea how I felt when Mrs Grady told me you'd collapsed?'

Jack groaned. 'It wasn't that serious.'

'It sounded serious to me. They kept you in the hospital for almost a week.'

'They were doing tests,' said Jack wearily. 'That's what doctors do. And I guess I'm an unusual subject.'

'So what happens now?'

Jack's mouth twisted. 'Yeah, that's the million-dollar question.'

Rachel frowned. 'What do you mean?'

'Well, face it, Rachel. I'm not the powerhouse you thought you married, am I? Maybe you ought to think twice about that divorce?'

Rachel caught her breath. 'That's ridiculous, and you know it. According to Mrs Grady there's every chance that you'll make a full recovery.' She gave him an impassioned look. 'You know, she warned me that you were feeling sorry for yourself, but I didn't realise how right she was.'

Her words sounded harsh, even to her own ears, but she had to shake him out of his apathy somehow. Did he really think she'd married him for any other reason than that she'd been madly in love with him? Dear God, she didn't care what he did so long as he was well and happy.

She knew she'd said too much when he rocked back on his heels and said drily, 'Thanks, Rachel. I knew I could rely on you to tell it like it is. What you see is what you get, right?'

'Stop it!'

She was alarmed now, but he wasn't listening to her. 'Yeah,' he said. 'You're right. I *am* feeling sorry for myself. Bloody sorry, as it goes.' He shook his head. 'You know, I thought I was pretty well invincible. I could be hurt, yeah, but physically I was strong. Then something like this comes along and you realise you've been kidding yourself. You're nothing special. Just human. That's all.'

Rachel sighed. 'We're all human, Jack.'

'Yeah, right.'

'Surely you realise you were doing too much?' She spread her hands. 'Lately, you were spending more and more time at the office, working every hour God sent. No wonder I thought you were having an affair. You used not to stay away all day and all night as well.'

Jack shrugged. 'I know.'

'But I'm not blaming you,' she hastened on, needing to get it said before she lost the courage to do so. 'I know I've been blind and selfish, thinking I was the only one who suffered when our babies died.' She gazed at him despairingly. 'I've thought about it a lot since—well, since the accident. It should have brought us closer together, but instead I let it drive us apart.'

'That's all water under the bridge now.'

'But it's important—don't you see?' Rachel insisted vehemently. 'If we—if *I* hadn't driven you away, Karen would never have been able to hurt us.'

'Right. Karen.' Jack was harsh. 'I wondered when we'd get around to her.'

Rachel bit her lip. 'She came here, you know. While you were in Ireland.' She shivered. 'She told me she'd been staying with your parents.'

'Yeah.' Jack made a weary sound. 'Mrs Grady told me.'

'But she hadn't?'

'Will you believe me if I say no?'

Rachel nodded.

'Okay. She was lying.' He took a steadying breath. 'She did turn up there. The same morning you did, as it happens.' A wry smile tugged at the corners of his mouth. 'My mother sent her packing.'

'So—so while we were—'

'Somewhere else?'

'—making love,' amended Rachel huskily. 'While we were at the pool, she was at your parents' cottage?'

'When you arrived, yeah,' agreed Jack flatly. 'I wanted to tell you, but I didn't want anything to spoil the day. And as it turned out it wasn't necessary. My mother had called a taxi for her and given her the fare back to Dublin.'

'Oh, God! Karen must have been so mad!' Rachel pressed suddenly cold hands to her cheeks. 'No wonder she—'

'No wonder she—what?'

Rachel shook her head. 'It doesn't matter.'

'Tell me!'

Rachel drew a breath. 'No wonder she—told me all those lies.'

'What lies?'

'About you; about the cottage. That was how she could describe it all in such detail. She must have been desperate when I told her I didn't believe her.'

Jack caught her arm, her skin soft and familiar beneath his hard fingers. 'You *told* her you didn't believe her?' he echoed roughly. 'Am I supposed to believe that?'

'It's the truth.' Rachel was eager to explain. 'Oh, I'll admit I wasn't sure what to believe at first. But—well, after I'd had time to think about it…' She looked up at him, her expression open and innocent. 'I just knew she was lying.'

'So why didn't you tell me?'

'How could I?' Rachel spoke appealingly. 'I—I had the accident, remember? I was pretty shook up for a while. Then—then I heard that you'd come back to England, and you hadn't even bothered to find out how I was. Lucy said—well, it seemed possible that you didn't care about me after all.'

'Lucy!' Jack's brows drew together as he absorbed what

she was saying. 'Perhaps it would have been easier if she'd told me you'd had the accident *before* I got back to England, hmm?'

Rachel nodded. Then, trying to be fair, she added, 'It wasn't her fault, really. George—George Thomas, that is—he assured her he'd phoned you.'

'Well, he hadn't.'

'I know that now. When—when Mrs Grady explained what had happened, I knew I had to see you.'

Jack's fingers gentled, his thumb massaging the sensitive veins on the inner side of her arm. 'Are you sure this isn't pity?' he demanded, still not convinced he wasn't imagining the whole thing. Goodness knew, he'd indulged in self-deception before. Like the night Rachel had taken him to bed...

'Why would I pity you?' she countered, lifting her hand to stroke the roughening skin of his jawline. 'I love you,' she added simply. 'I've never stopped loving you.'

Jack was stunned. It was what he'd dreamed of, what he'd prayed for, and yet now that it had happened he couldn't take it in. After everything Karen had done, after all her efforts to split them up, he still couldn't believe it was over.

'You do still love me?' Rachel prompted, his continued silence beginning to worry her, and he expelled a shaky breath.

'Need you ask?' he got out thickly and unable to wait a moment longer, Rachel put her hand behind his head and pulled his face down to hers.

He needed no second bidding. His lips took possession of hers with a hungry urgency and Rachel leaned into him, opening her mouth like a flower to the sun.

'God,' he muttered unsteadily as he felt the soft pressure of her breasts against his chest. His hands captured her shoulders, pulling her even closer, so that the growing bulge in his pants was cushioned against the warmth of her stomach.

He rubbed himself against her, loving the way her legs parted automatically to allow him to wedge his thigh between them. And if he was dizzy now, it was the mindless dizziness of knowing that nothing and no one could come between them again.

'Jack…' she breathed, when he released her mouth to tip the strap of her vest off her shoulder and nuzzle the creamy slopes of her breasts. His tongue traced the line of her cleavage before he dipped one hand inside her bra and let the hard nub of her nipple push into his palm.

'I want you,' he said hoarsely, cupping her breasts in hands that trembled a little. 'You're everything I've ever wanted,' he added, his mouth finding hers again with increasing urgency. 'Let's go upstairs.'

And then the doorbell rang.

CHAPTER FOURTEEN

'DON'T ANSWER IT!'

Rachel clung to Jack's arm, one leg hooked about his calf, and he was tempted. He wanted her. God, he was consumed by the need to lose himself again in the smouldering heat of her body. But someone was at the door; someone who, as the doorbell pealed again, obviously knew he was at home.

'I've got to,' he groaned, feeling an instinctive sense of deprivation as he moved away from her. 'It could be the doctor.'

'Dr Moore?'

'The same,' he agreed, fastening the button at his waist, which Rachel had loosened, with some regret. 'He's taken to checking up on me from time to time. Wait here.' He urged her back into the den, the stubble on his jaw scraping her chin as he stole another breath-robbing kiss. 'I'll get rid of him.'

Rachel nodded, the hand she'd used to clutch the front of his shirt falling to her side as he crossed the hall. 'Don't be long.'

Jack didn't say anything, but the look he cast back at her was eloquent with meaning, and Rachel's stomach gave a nervous little flip. Then, responding to his suggestion, she stepped back into the den.

But only so far. She stayed just inside the door, so she'd be able to hear who it was. And, although she knew she had no reason to feel apprehensive now, she couldn't help the twinge of foreboding she felt when Jack opened the door.

'George!'

Jack's greeting was less than enthusiastic. Recent events had caused him to re-evaluate what his mother had said about George, and he now had his own ideas about the other man's role in all of this. He'd actually been putting off the confrontation he'd known was to come—not least because of the way George had kept the news of Rachel's accident from him. But now was definitely not the time to get into that.

'Jack!'

In his polished Oxford boots and pinstripe suit, George had evidently come straight from the office, and Jack wondered what had induced him to call this afternoon. Apart from a couple of phone calls that Mrs Grady had fielded he'd made no attempt to see him since his return, and it made Jack wonder if he had a line to Lucy Robards and knew about her trip to London. And the fact that Rachel would be alone and might come here…

'Hey, man.' Was it only his imagination, or was George's greeting a little too hearty? He held out his hand and Jack was virtually obliged to take it. 'It's good to see you.'

'Is it?' Jack withdrew his hand as soon as he could, surreptitiously wiping it on his jeans as he did so. George's palm had been hot and sweaty. There was no doubt about it, he was on edge, and Jack wondered why. 'What are you doing here, George?'

'What do you think?' George's plump face was flushed and his smile was definitely suspect. He ran a nervous hand over his balding scalp. 'I've been concerned about you, Jack. Aren't you going to invite me in?'

'Oh, well…' Jack gave a rueful smile in return. 'It's a bit awkward at the moment, George. You see, I've got company.'

George's jaw dropped. 'She's here?' he exclaimed in dismay, and although Jack was tempted to tease him some more, something about George's attitude made him think again.

'Where else did you think she'd be?' he queried tersely, his brows drawing together. 'She lives here. Where else would she be?'

'Oh!' George's expression seemed to clear. 'I see.' He licked his lips. 'You mean Rachel. Of course, of course,' he added, pulling out a white handkerchief and mopping his brow. 'My, it's a warm afternoon, isn't it?'

'Wet and warm,' agreed Jack drily, allowing himself a glance over his shoulder. Mmm, he thought, he could think of something else that was wet and warm. Or should that be wet and hot? Whatever, it was infinitely more appealing than standing here listening to George.

Impatience giving an edge to his voice, he said. 'Is that all, then? As you can see, I'm feeling pretty good right now.'

'Excellent.' George put his handkerchief away again. 'So—what's the prognosis? When are we going to see you back in the office?'

'That depends.' Jack shrugged. 'Not immediately, obviously. I'm thinking of taking Rachel on a prolonged second honeymoon as soon as she can get away.'

'Get away?' George frowned.

'Yes. She's got commitments, too.'

George hesitated. 'I—well, I have to be honest, I didn't realise you two were back together,' he said, running a finger around the inside of his collar. 'I mean, the last I heard she was staying with that friend of hers—Lucy Robards.'

Jack stiffened. 'You know Lucy?'

'Only by reputation,' said George hastily. 'Her column and so on. But I believe she's quite a feisty woman.'

'And where did you hear that Rachel was staying with Lucy? Did *she* tell you?'

George shifted from foot to foot. 'She might have done. I'm not sure where I heard it. But it's common knowledge in the office.'

'Is it?' Jack could feel himself getting angry, but if nothing else his illness had taught him that anger was not the way to go. 'I suppose if you've had a near-fatal accident you need people who care about you around you.' He paused. 'Of course, *I* didn't know about it. No one bothered to tell me.'

'No?' George succeeded in looking scandalised. 'You mean the Robards woman didn't let you know?'

'Apparently not.' Jack had to suppress the urge to bury his fist in George's smug face. 'Funny, that. She told Rachel that *you'd* offered to do it.'

'No!' George gave an indignant gasp. 'I'm sure I didn't say any such thing.' But then, as if he felt the need to cover all the bases, he added quickly, 'In any case, I might have hesitated to do it. I mean, no one wanted to hinder your recovery, Jack.'

Jack regarded him sceptically. 'Well, you'll be happy to know your—er—consideration has been duly noted. Oh, and just for the record, Rachel and I have never been apart.'

Rachel, standing in the doorway of the den, listening, felt a glow of satisfaction envelop her. She badly wanted to go and join them, to tell George Thomas what she thought of his sneaky behaviour, to accuse him of doing his best to split her and Jack up.

But George was speaking again, tension evident in his voice. 'You're a lucky man,' he said tightly. 'I've always thought so.'

'Have you, George?' Jack could have left it there, but something drove him to say, 'Even when Karen Johnson was accusing me of being the father of her child?' His derision came through. 'Come on—surely no one would envy me that?'

'Perhaps not.' George squared his shoulders. 'But you know, Jack, there are people who would say you deserved everything you got.'

Rachel caught her breath. But the denial she waited for didn't come. However, George must have seen something in Jack's face to trouble him, because he went on in quite a different tone. 'I mean...' she could hear the defensive note in his voice... 'if you hadn't taken her out, made her think you liked her, she'd probably have had the abortion and been done with it.'

There was a pregnant pause after that statement, and then Jack said quietly, 'You think she was considering an abortion, George?'

The other man cleared his throat. 'How would I know what she was thinking?' he exclaimed, and again he sounded defensive. 'I can't read her mind, Jack. It was you she wanted, not me.'

'Was it?'

The significance of what those two words implied hit Rachel like a thunderbolt. My God, she thought incredulously, Jack thinks *George* is the father of Karen's baby. She blinked. But George was happily married. He had three teenage daughters, for goodness' sake. Yet the fact that he was married hadn't stopped Karen from accusing Jack, had it?

The sound of another car turning into the drive distracted all of them. It came to a skidding halt on the forecourt, gravel spraying from beneath its wheels. A door opened and was slammed shut, then another voice—one that Rachel had hoped never to hear again—exclaimed shrilly, 'Well, well—George. What's this? A pre-emptive strike?'

Rachel had heard enough. She wasn't going to hide away like a frightened mouse while that woman invaded her home for a third time. Checking that the button on her shorts was fastened, and running combing fingers through her hair, she left the den and started across the hall to the open doorway.

Meanwhile, George was saying harshly, 'What the devil are you doing here, Karen?'

'I could ask *you* that,' she retorted, coming to join them on the porch. 'I wondered where you were going and I followed you.' She gave a scornful snort. 'Surprise, surprise— you came straight here.'

George glared at her and Jack realised that that was who George had really meant when he'd asked if *she* was here. Not Rachel. Karen!

'You have no right to come here, Karen,' George went on aggressively. 'You're not welcome. I'd have thought Jack would have convinced you of that by now.'

'This isn't about Jack,' said Karen angrily, her expression darkening ominously when Rachel came to slip a hand through her husband's arm. 'And what's *she* doing here?' she added, almost mimicking the words George had used. 'You told me she and Jack were living apart.'

'I don't recall telling you any such thing,' muttered George, with obvious discomfort. But Karen wasn't having that.

'Oh, you did,' she insisted. 'As I remember it, you said that when she got out of hospital she went to stay with that friend of hers in the village.' Her lips twisted as she looked at Rachel. 'George told me you'd had a nasty fall.'

Jack felt Rachel's nails dig into his wrist, but she didn't say anything, and, feeling an immense desire to protect her, he said, 'George always did get things wrong.' He paused. 'You should have had more sense than to believe him, Karen. I'm sure he's let you down before.'

'Look, I don't have time for this,' said George, evidently wishing he were anywhere else than here. 'I'm pleased you're feeling so much better, Jack. And Rachel. It's good to see you, too.' He turned to Karen and took hold of her arm. 'Come on, Karen. It's obvious we're in the way. Let me see you to your car.'

'Let go of me.' In spite of the bulkiness of her body, Karen shook him off easily. 'I'm not going anywhere. Not until I know what you've been telling Jack about me.'

George's dismay was obvious. 'I haven't told Jack anything about you, you silly girl,' he protested, trying and failing to make her take his hand. 'For pity's sake, can't you see you're just embarrassing everyone?'

'The only person I'm embarrassing is you, George.' Karen retorted scornfully. Then, turning to Jack, she went on, 'Don't let him fool you. He has his own agenda. Since he discovered *she*—' Rachel shivered as Karen's cold eyes assessed her '—was all right, he's been wetting himself that you might connect the dots.'

'What dots?'

'Karen—'

Ignoring George's agonised cry, Karen gave Rachel a contemptuous look. 'I don't know what Jacks sees in you,' she said coldly. 'What a pity that old man saved your life.'

'That's enough!' Jack spoke harshly. Then, looking at George, he said again, 'What are these dots she's talking about?'

George groaned. 'You tell me,' he said. 'Don't listen to her, Jack. You can't believe a word she says.'

'He can't believe a word *you* say,' Karen contradicted him. She looked at Jack again. 'George knew how I felt about you. He's always known. But that didn't stop him from seducing me. And then, when I got pregnant, he used my love for you to try and save his own miserable skin!'

'Love!' George sneered. 'You don't know the meaning of the word.'

'And you do?' Karen snorted. 'Give me a break! It was your idea to tell Jack it was his baby. Just because I'd confided in you about him spending that night at my house.'

George's eyes moved from Jack's to Karen's and back again. 'She's crazy!' he exclaimed. 'You told me yourself she'd been stalking you. You can't believe I'd want any part of her—'

He broke off as Karen's hand connected with his cheek, and Rachel saw the marks of her fingers white against George's flushed skin. 'You bastard!' Karen cried. 'You wanted me. You wanted me because you thought Jack might want me. Then, when he didn't, you thought you'd use me to ruin his life.'

'This is ludicrous—'

George tried again, but once again Karen overrode him. 'Why do you think Rachel turned up at Ballyryan on the same day I did?' she demanded, turning back to Jack. 'It was because your good friend George suggested it.'

Rachel's mouth felt dry. 'George...?'

'She's lying,' he persisted desperately. 'Can't you see that? She's already tried these tricks on your husband, and now, because that didn't work, she's blaming me!'

This time Karen let him have his say. 'Somehow,' she said casually, 'I don't think Rachel will believe you. After what happened to her.' Her eyes on the other girl's were full of malice. 'After that, she has to know I wouldn't have done what I did unless I was desperate.'

'And what *did* you do, Karen?' Jack demanded, ignoring George's attempt to dissuade him. 'Come on. I want to know.'

'You mean she didn't tell you?' Karen gave a short laugh. 'Poor Rachel! Were you afraid it was Jack who made me push you off the cliff?'

'Why didn't you tell me?'

It was some time later, and although Jack had wanted to call the police, Rachel had persuaded him to let both of them go. She didn't think she could bear to face the horror of her fall all over again, and besides, she didn't think anyone had forced Karen to do what she did.

In many ways it was a relief to know that she hadn't imagined that push, that awful moment when she'd known there was no way she could save herself. Karen had seen an opportunity to rid herself of her rival once and for all, but at the end of the day, it would just be Rachel's word against hers. She'd admitted nothing, and it was George who was going to have to handle the fallout from her other revelations.

Rachel sighed. They were in the bedroom they'd shared for the first three years of their marriage. In the middle of George's attempt to defend himself against Karen's accusations Mrs Grady had returned—on foot—and Rachel, for one, had been grateful for the reprieve.

'How could I expect you to believe me when I'd been so unwilling to believe you?' she asked simply now, standing at the window, her back to the room. 'Dear God, Jack, there had been so many misunderstandings between us. I just wanted to put Karen and the past behind us.'

'But she could have killed you,' muttered Jack hoarsely, moving to stand behind her. He laid possessive hands on her shoulders. 'What am I saying? She did almost kill you. If that man hadn't been walking his dog—'

'Don't.' Rachel trembled. 'I've had nightmares for weeks. Ever since it happened, actually. I just want to forget all about it.'

'I won't forget,' said Jack thickly, tipping the straps of her vest off her shoulders and bending to bestow a lingering kiss on her soft skin. 'You're the most precious thing in the world to me. When I think that I could have lost you because of that woman's—'

'It's over, Jack.' Rachel turned now, shaking her arms free of the fallen straps and putting them round his neck. 'We're together again. And nothing and no one can drive us apart.'

'You'd better believe it.'

Jack's lips turned against the side of her neck, his tongue tracing a sensuous path from the erratic pulse that beat below her ear to the creamy slopes of her breasts. Nudging the silk vest lower, he captured one rosy nipple through her bra, rolling it against his tongue and tugging gently with his teeth.

Rachel's senses swam. Her bra was wet now, and clinging to her hot skin, and although Jack was being gentle, she sensed the urgency he was trying so hard to control.

She guessed he thought she was still in a state of shock, fragile, liable to break into a thousand pieces if he was too rough with her.

How wrong he was!

'I want you,' she breathed, unclipping her bra and allowing her swollen breasts to spill into his hands. 'Let's go to bed.'

Jack expelled an unsteady breath. His own head was swimming, but it was a good feeling. Nothing like the dizziness he'd suffered before. Just being with Rachel again, knowing that she still loved him after everything that had happened, gave him an incredible feeling of satisfaction. He loved her so much, and for so long he'd been sure he'd lost her.

'And what if Mrs Grady comes to see if we want supper?' he asked huskily as Rachel allowed her bra and vest to fall to the floor in a delicious heap of apricot silk and lace.

'She won't,' said Rachel confidently, kicking off her shorts and revealing herself in only a skimpy pair of bikini briefs. She hooked a nail into the waistband of his jeans. 'Don't you think you're a little overdressed?'

Jack needed no further encouragement. Stripping off his tee shirt and jeans, he revealed exactly how aroused he was. Meanwhile, Rachel scrambled onto the bed, spreading her arms and legs for his delectation.

'Hey, now who's overdressed?' Jack protested, crawling onto the bed beside her, and Rachel drew up one leg in knowing provocation.

'I thought you might like to do it,' she murmured, and Jack knelt beside her, sweeping his hand down over her breasts and the slight mound of her stomach to the elasticated waist of her briefs.

'My pleasure,' he breathed, lowering his head and using his teeth to pull the satin fabric down over her hips. 'Mmm, that's much better,' he approved, burying his face in the moist curls at the top of her legs. He breathed deeply. 'You know, I could get off on just the scent of you.'

Rachel quivered. 'My God, Jack, please—'

'Please what?' he asked, spreading her legs and slipping two fingers inside her. 'Don't you like this?' He felt the gush of heat that wet his hand and smiled. 'I thought I was pleasing you. You're certainly pleasing me.'

'Jack—'

Her balled fists beat the mattress at either side of his bent head and he gave a low, triumphant laugh. 'Okay,' he chided her softly. 'I know what you want.' He moved to kneel between her legs, teasing the entrance to her vagina with the tip of his erection. 'You want to play.'

'No,' she groaned, reaching for him imploringly. 'I want you.' Her eyes begged him not to waste any more time, and with a sigh of submission he slid sleekly into her sheath.

'Better?' he whispered against her mouth, and she trembled violently beneath him.

'Much—much better,' she answered, her nails digging into his broad shoulders. 'Just—just do it, Jack. Please…'

He made love to her with all the pent-up emotion they'd both suffered these past weeks. Fast and furious at first, but then slowly, sensuously, drawing out each moment until she was desperate and clinging to him again.

He silenced the ecstatic cries she made with his mouth, reluctant to draw back from her even for a second. They

were together again; they were whole. And for the first
time since that morning at St. Michaels pool, Jack felt as
if the future was something he could face without fear or
recrimination…

EPILOGUE

SIX months later, Jack was heading for the hospital again. But not because of his own health.

The night before, his wife had given birth to their first child, and, although he'd been with her every step of the way, eventually he'd been advised to go home and give his wife and son time to rest.

Jack had been reluctant to leave, but he'd known he had matters to attend to. Not least calling his mother and father and giving them the good news. And letting Mrs Grady know, of course. But, as she'd been there when Rachel had gone into labour, she wouldn't be quite so surprised.

For his part, Jack still found it hard to believe that he was a father at last. As soon as he and Rachel had got back together again he'd insisted on using protection when they made love. He hadn't wanted her to suffer another miscarriage. But, unknown to either of them, it had already been too late.

All those stomach upsets Rachel had had while she was staying with Lucy, the sickness that she'd put down to nerves and apprehension in the aftermath of Karen's violence, had had an entirely different cause. But it hadn't been until they were enjoying their second honeymoon in the Caribbean that a doctor, treating her for suspected heat-stroke, had diagnosed her condition.

By then Rachel had been estimated to be at least fifteen weeks into term—well beyond the point at which she'd miscarried in the past. According to Dr Lopez, there would be no reason to worry. Rachel was in good health and the baby's heartbeat was strong. So long as she didn't do anything too outrageous, there was no reason why she shouldn't have a healthy child.

Of course Jack had been both anxious and elated. Anxious that Rachel might blame him if anything went wrong, yet elated at the prospect of them becoming parents at last.

He needn't have worried. Rachel had been delighted and optimistic. Dr Lopez had given her the confidence to believe in herself again.

And there'd been no hitches—no problems other than the normal ones of unusual cravings and late-night feasts. Not only that, Rachel had felt so well during her pregnancy that she'd continued to work right up until the last few days.

Then, last night, baby James Riordan had been born—all of eight pounds in weight and robustly healthy. Rachel had been tired afterwards, of course, but she'd been immensely proud of her achievement. And such a beautiful mother, thought Jack happily. He hadn't been able to take his eyes off her.

Well, except when he'd held his son, he admitted honestly. Baby James looked amazingly like him, and, although he'd been too modest to comment on it, Rachel had pointed it out with a dimple of pride.

'Let's hope he doesn't break as many hearts as his father,' she'd whispered teasingly, when Jack had laid the baby back in her arms. 'But he is handsome, isn't he, Jack?' She'd looked up at him. 'I've always thought you were a beautiful man.'

Jack had wanted to kiss her then, but he'd contented himself with a tender stroke of her cheek. 'I'll remind you of that when you get home,' he'd said softly, mindful of the nurse's watching eyes. 'I'll be back soon. Get some sleep.'

Jack's parents had been delighted and eager to meet the new arrival. They'd promised to fly over at the end of the week, after Rachel had had a few days to recover her strength. Then, a couple of months after that, Jack, Rachel, and the baby would be relocating to Ireland for six months. Taking his father's advice, Jack had been renovating the old Ryan House, and although it wasn't exactly as he wanted it yet, he'd have plenty of time to make the final changes while they were living there.

There was a new arrangement at Fox Construction, too. Not without some regret, Jack had had to find himself a new manager, and David Coleman would be in charge of the company while Jack was away. He was hoping to spend half the year in England and half in Ireland from now on, keeping in touch with the office when he needed to through online conferencing and email.

The really sad thing as far as Jack was concerned was that George's wife was divorcing him. Learning he'd had an affair had shocked and hurt her, but finding out about Karen's imminent confinement had destroyed all trust between them. The last thing he and Rachel had heard was that George, Karen, and their new baby daughter were now living in London. George's wife had contacted a solicitor, and his three teenage daughters were refusing to speak to their father at present.

For his part, Jack's health had never been better. He'd had a comprehensive check-up a few weeks ago, and according to Dr Moore his arrhythmia had corrected itself. So long as he took more care of himself—something Rachel insisted she'd attend to from now on—he should have no more worries.

The change of lifestyle had definitely helped. That, and knowing that his and Rachel's love for one another was stronger than ever. Having the baby was the fulfillment of all their hopes, and they were a real family at last.

It had been agreed that they'd employ a nanny before they left for Ireland. Rachel wanted to go on working, and happily there was a summer house in the garden of the house in Ballyryan that Jack had taken great pleasure in redesigning as a studio for his wife.

Their only concern had been that Mrs Grady might find the upheaval in her life too much to handle. Having to move between homes on a regular basis for the foreseeable future might daunt her, and they'd be devastated to lose her.

However, Mrs Grady had been excited at the prospect of living in Ballyryan. She'd never been to Ireland, she'd said, and it was a country she very much wanted to visit. Besides, she'd added incorrigibly, who else was going to keep the nanny in order when Rachel was working?

The gates of St. Luke's Hospital loomed ahead, and Jack drove between them. Then, after finding himself a parking space, he gathered up a huge bouquet of flowers, bags of clothes for both Rachel and the baby, and the car-friendly carrycot which his son would occupy for the journey back to Market Abbas, and headed for the entrance.

The maternity ward was on the top floor, and he contained his patience and took the lift like any responsible adult. His inclination was to vault up the stairs, but recent experience had taught him to be wary. At least for the present.

He encountered the ward sister at the nursing station, and she escorted him to his wife's room. 'Mrs Riordan has had a decent night's sleep and she can't wait to go home,' she said with a cheerful smile. 'Do you think you can cope?'

'Go home? Today?'

Jack's apprehension must have shown, because the nurse gave him a reassuring pat on the arm. 'Don't worry,' she said, as they reached Rachel's door. 'Babies aren't half as fragile as they appear.' She opened the door, assured herself that her patient was awake, and then ushered him into the room.

Rachel was reclining against the pillows, but she was wearing the turquoise silk dressing gown she'd brought in with her and Jack realised she'd already been out of bed. Baby James was asleep in his cot beside the bed. Although Rachel had been lying studying her son, at Jack's entrance she immediately sat up and held out her arms to him.

'Hey,' he said huskily, setting down the things he'd brought up from the car and coming to perch on the side of the bed. 'How are you? Both?'

'We're fine,' Rachel answered softly, slipping her arms about his neck. 'Did you hear? We can come home today.'

'Yeah. I heard.' Jack returned the kiss she bestowed on his parted lips with interest. 'Are you sure you're going to be all right?'

'Mmm.' Rachel nodded, the lapels of her robe parting as she leant towards him. She glanced down at herself and then up at him rather shyly. 'James had his first feed this morning. From me, I mean.' She took an uneven breath. 'It was—awesome!'

Jack's eyes darkened. 'I'm jealous.'

'You don't have to be.' She was delightful in her eager-ness to reassure him. 'I love James. Of course I do. But I love his father more than I can ever say.'

'Try,' said Jack gruffly, unable to resist burying his face in the soft hollow of her neck. 'God, you smell good.' He nipped her with his teeth. 'And taste good, too.'

Rachel dimpled and looked beyond him. 'Are those for me?' She indicated the flowers. 'They're beautiful, but we'll have to take them home again.'

'The ward sister can have them,' said Jack, cupping her face in his hands and staring at her hungrily. 'I'll get you some more. After we get home.'

Rachel nodded. 'All right.' She caught her lower lip be-tween her teeth. 'By the way, Lucy rang this morning.'

'Oh, did she?' Relations between Rachel and her friend had been tense ever since his wife had learned that Lucy had suspected George Thomas hadn't made the call to Ireland. But he refused to let the other woman spoil his mood.

'Yes.' Rachel touched his mouth with her finger. 'Apparently she'd rung the house to tell me she's leaving for London next week. Mrs Grady had to tell her where I was and—well, she congratulated us. You don't mind, do you?'

Jack grimaced. 'I guess not.'

'Good.' Rachel didn't want to talk about Lucy either, but something had to be said. 'I mean, I know you two never hit it off, but she was there for me when I needed her. I don't think we'll ever be friends again, but I'm glad she's making a success of her career.'

'You're a very generous woman,' said Jack gently, smoothing his thumbs over her eyebrows. 'And I love you so very much. I'm never going to let you go.'

'That's good. Because I feel the same,' she said, pressing herself against him. 'And now, because our son is stirring and I have to get dressed, would you like to pick him up?'

A Special Offer from

HARLEQUIN Presents

She's in his bedroom,
but he can't buy her love....

Showered with diamonds,
draped in exquisite lingerie,
whisked around the world...

**The ultimate fantasy becomes a reality
in Harlequin Presents!**

When Nora Lang acquires some business
information that top tycoon Blake Macleod
can't risk being leaked, he must keep Nora
in his sight.... He'll make love to her for
the whole weekend!

MISTRESS FOR
A WEEKEND
by Susan Napier

Book #2569,

on sale September 2006

www.eHarlequin.com   HPMTM0906